GUILT TRIP

Also by Anne Cassidy:

ANNE CASSIDY

GUILT TRIP

■SCHOLASTIC

First published in the UK in 2010 by Scholastic Children's Books
An imprint of Scholastic Ltd
Euston House, 24 Eversholt Street
London, NW1 1DB, UK
Registered office: Westfield Road, Southam, Warwickshire, CV47 0RA
SCHOLASTIC and associated logos are trademarks and/or
registered trademarks of Scholastic Inc.

ISBN 978 1407 11070 7

A CIP catalogue record for this book is available
from the British Library.

Printed in the UK by CPI Group (UK) Ltd, Croydon, CR0 4YY
Papers used by Scholastic Children's Books are made from
wood grown in sustainable forests.

5 7 9 10 8 6 4

www.scholastic.co.uk/zone

ONE

Year Thirteen

Alison couldn't believe it when she heard that Jackson was back. Hannah Cunningham rang and told her. The phone call had been a total surprise. It had been a long time since she'd seen the name *Hannah* on her mobile.

"One of the girls from the salon saw him. She said he looked thin and pale. She thought he looked anorexic."

"When was this?" Alison said.

"Yesterday," Hannah said. "I thought I'd let you know."

"Why me?"

"Oh come on, you and him were close. I always knew that."

Alison could hear the noise from Hannah's mum's hairdresser's in the background. Music playing. Voices calling out. A television programme. She struggled for something to say.

"It's nearly two years since Daniel died," Hannah said.

"I know."

"I can't help thinking about it. You know – the awful way he died."

"I know."

"Do you ever think about it?"

"Sometimes."

The phone call ended soon after and Alison placed her mobile on her desk in between her folders and her books and her revision schedule.

Was Jackson back?

There had been other times in the last two years when people in school had said that they'd seen Jackson, but it had never come to anything. Alison had been anxious on each occasion but Jackson had not reappeared. Then Alison had felt a mix of emotions: sadness tinged with relief.

Did she ever think about the way Daniel Feeny died?

She almost laughed at the *idea* of the question. She thought about it every day. Every hour. It was always with her.

No one should die in the way that he had died.

She wasn't surprised that Hannah still thought about it. Hannah had cried a lot after they found Daniel's body. She had looked puffy-eyed and red-faced for weeks. Months later, when Alison passed her in college or saw her in the refectory, Hannah had looked pale and serious, as if she didn't laugh very much. She dropped out of her NVQ hairdressing course for a while, and then Alison saw her with a lad on the broadway. She had finally got on with her life. There was no reason why she shouldn't.

She knew nothing about the death of Daniel Feeny.

It was only Alison and Stephen and Jackson who knew.

Alison got up early the morning after the call from Hannah. She put on her running clothes and pulled her trainers on. It was Saturday, so that meant eight kilometres. Downstairs, she filled her water bottle and picked her mobile up, sticking it into the bumbag she carried while running. She stood tall and stretched her arms up to the ceiling. Then she lifted each leg and flexed it. She moved her shoulders and her neck and let her arms hang loosely, shaking her hands. After finishing her warm-up exercises, she looked at her watch. Eight kilometres should take about forty minutes. That meant she should be back in time to do some work on her assignment before going to the charity shop.

She left the house and ran along the road. As she got into her stride, the rhythm of her steps relaxed her. One foot after the other, passing number 56, number 62, number 74, the white van, the black Nissan, the green Fiat, turning left, heading out of the estate, towards Blackwood Park and open ground. Her breathing was regular: inhale, exhale, one foot down, the other foot down, inhale, exhale.

By the time she got to the path around the lake, her body was on autopilot.

Why would Jackson come back? After all this time?

She glanced to the side and saw the lake shimmering in the early-morning sun. There was no one around. Not even the odd dog-walker. She ran on, feeling the heat of the sun between her shoulder blades. In the distance was the end of the lake and the halfway point of her run.

The last time she'd actually seen Jackson was after the funeral. They'd all been there in the back row of the church. Stephen Grainger was in his dark suit and wore his sunglasses right the way through the service. Hannah was with her mum, the two of them looking like sisters, Hannah's skirt a couple of inches shorter than her mum's. Alison wore black trousers and a white blouse. She'd ironed them both the previous evening and put them on a hanger. She'd had to polish her school shoes so that they looked respectable. Along the row had been some other kids from school. They nudged each other and fidgeted through the service as though they didn't want to be there.

Jackson had turned up late. When the church door creaked, they'd all looked round. Jackson appeared to be wearing the same clothes that he'd had on for days. He had stubble and circles under his eyes. He shuffled along the row and sat beside her. She put her hand on his arm. Jackson didn't respond. He seemed lifeless.

When the service was over and they were all standing outside, Mr Feeny came over to them. *You were real friends for Daniel*, he said. *Thank you for coming.*

Jackson's face was the colour of a wax candle. His mouth was twisted and for one heart-stopping moment Alison thought that he was going to say something to Mr Feeny. Instead he turned and walked off down the road. She watched him as he got further and further away.

Soon after he'd left to go and live in Brighton with his brother. He hadn't said goodbye. Not a word.

She came to the furthest point of the lake and slowed down, each step getting shorter than the last. She finally stopped and stood still, her breaths becoming louder. She could feel her heart thumping in her chest like an engine winding down. She unzipped her bumbag and took out her bottle of water. She took a gulp and then poured some into the cup of her hand and splashed it over her face. She walked over to the bench and sat down, her elbows on her knees, and stared ahead.

The lake was peaceful. The surface was flat like a mirror. A single duck moved nearby and it sent out slow-motion ripples. She watched them get bigger and bigger until they disappeared into the water and the lake settled again.

During the day it was busy. There were boats on it, and children and families had picnics in the grounds. Sometimes, away from the lake, there were big games of football or cricket, or kids would bring their tennis racquets and play on the grass. On summer evenings, if the weather was good, groups of teenagers would gather and sit for hours smoking and drinking lager, cider or wine, playing games and pairing off as the daylight sank away and the darkness crept up.

Alison had enjoyed evenings like that. She and other kids from her class lazing round looking for members of the opposite sex. Then she lay back on the grass and felt the earth as it seemed to hum beneath her. Feeling woozy from drink, she stared up at the sky, still and deep like an ocean. The light from the moon shone like gossamer across the blue-black of space. Everything was before her. When she was young.

That was before she met Stephen and they started driving round in his car. Before Hannah and Jackson joined them and they became a foursome. Before they got involved with Daniel Feeny.

Now, in the early morning, there were usually only a couple of people with their dogs round the lake. Looking to the other end, she thought she could see one now. By the time she ran back along the other side of the lake there would be a few people, a number of dogs, a car or two making its way along the lane to get to the sports centre.

She began to run again, slowly at first and then pushing harder as she passed by familiar landmarks: the thicket, the picnic tables, the wooden building that housed the café, the boats moored along the edge. She looked up from time to time and saw the dog-walker still at the other end. She was tiring and felt herself slowing down, but instead she lowered her head, her eyes looking at the path, and forced herself to keep going. She made herself think of other things: her essay that had to be finished by Monday, the bookshelves in the charity shop that she had decided to reorganize, her promised visit to her gran's that evening. She was busy. These days she was always busy. She glanced up and saw the dog-walker again. This time she noticed that there wasn't a dog nearby.

She slowed her pace. She was tired anyway but a feeling of trepidation was pulling at her back. When she got closer she looked again, squinting into the sunlight trying to work out if there was a dog, a small dog, maybe hidden by the long grass. There wasn't, and within a few paces she recognized the figure in front of her and her heart seemed to fold in on itself.

Hannah had been right.

Ryan Jackson was back.

That night the ghost came. It was the first time for months, maybe six months. She'd gone straight to sleep, tired after a day in the charity shop and a night round her gran's. She'd hardly had a moment to think about Jackson – at least, she hadn't allowed herself a moment. Before she went to bed she drank two big tumblers of red wine.

When she opened her eyes the darkness was thick and black. It took a moment for her to know that she was awake and not in a state of dreaming. Her eyelids flickered, her mouth felt dry and her head heavy. It was warm but she pulled the covers around her and pushed her face into the pillow.

Then she heard it.

The whimpering. Tiny high cries that came from behind her. She stiffened herself, made herself solid and tight, but still she felt the old chill, the old fear, rising out of her chest like a vapour.

The noise was low and urgent. She listened keenly to each sound. Sometimes it was hardly audible or human, more like a defeated dog. Tonight it came from the corner of her room where her desk was.

The room was hot and she wanted to throw off the

covers, to open the window to let the air in, but she didn't dare. She lay still, nothing moving, sipping her breath through her mouth.

The cries became louder, almost like words, and she listened to them with a rising panic. It was always like this, but that didn't make it any easier. The cries always got louder before they died away. One final heart-rending whimper and then there was quiet.

Afterwards she lay for ages, for hours it seemed, until she was sure that it had gone. Then she slid out from under the covers and sat up. She switched the light on and felt the darkness back off into the edges of the room.

She looked round.

Nothing.

The dryness in her throat felt like grit. She swallowed a few times.

Jackson was back, and so was her ghost.

TWO

Year Eleven

Ali wished that Stephen would shut up. No one was interested in his VW Golf GTI Turbo. No one. She looked across the table at Hannah, who was picking the remaining crumbs of a muffin from its pleated wrapper. Jackson, Hannah's boyfriend, was staring at the screen of his mobile, nodding politely from time to time at what Stephen was saying. Ali pulled a strip from her napkin and glanced out of the window of the service café. It was overcast, the sky crammed with puffy clouds. A couple of hours before, when they started out, the sky had been sharp blue and the sun butter yellow.

"Are we going up to Blackwood or not?" Hannah said.

"If we have to," Stephen said.

"You said we would," Ali said.

"I don't care one way or another," Jackson said.

"Oh, let's go then. I'll just have a slash," Stephen said, getting up and walking away.

"I'm going to the loo," Hannah said, sorting through her bag and pulling out a large make-up case.

Ali watched Stephen stride off towards the toilets and Hannah follow him. She'd left her bag on the seat. It had pink and white candy stripes on it and it was bursting with stuff that Hannah always carried with her: spare shoes, make-up, hairbrush, jacket, tissues, novel. They'd only been for a ride to Southend and back, but Hannah had taken enough stuff for a weekend away. She looked up and saw that Jackson was staring at the bag as well. He caught her eye and they both smiled.

"What does she carry in that bag?" he said.

They'd both been thinking the same thing. It wasn't the first time. She and Jackson often seemed to be in agreement about things. Ali noticed a leather band on his wrist. She reached over and touched it with her finger.

"Is that new?" she said.

"Yep."

"It's nice."

"Hannah thinks it's too girly."

"I like it."

"Did I see you coming out of Mrs Caine's office the other day?"

Ali nodded. "She's my university mentor. She's been seeing me on and off this year about my plans."

"You're only doing GCSEs. Applying for university is over a year away."

"Yes, but she wants me to apply for Cambridge. She's been mentoring me, you know, about working hard, getting high grades, aiming for a top university."

"Is that what you want?"

Ali shrugged. "Don't know. Mum and Dad want it. How about you?"

"Going to Brighton. My brother Mark? He's bought this run-down place there and I'm helping him renovate it. I can live there while I do my degree. Won't cost me anything."

She heard her name being called and looked round to see Stephen standing by the edge of the tables. He had his car keys in his hand as if he was getting ready for a quick getaway.

"Probably going to do history. What about you?"

"English, I think."

Jackson looked like he had more to say. She would have liked to tell him about the courses that Mrs Caine had shown her, but there wasn't time. Stephen was waiting and any minute Hannah would come back. They rarely spoke about stuff like this when they were in a foursome.

"Time to go," she said, reaching across the table and picking up Hannah's candy-striped bag.

The three of them stood by the exit doors and waited.

"Where is she?" Jackson said, under his breath.

"Probably doing her hair," Ali said.

Stephen's ringtone sounded. He held his phone up and looked at the screen.

"Jonesy," he said, explaining, opening a text.

She watched him, his eyes narrowed in concentration, as he tapped out an answer to his text. She couldn't help but focus on the scar that ran down the right side of his face. Mostly she'd stopped noticing it, but just now it seemed ragged and untidy, like a line drawn with an unsteady hand. It reminded her of the first time she'd mentioned Stephen to her friends in school.

There's this guy who's just moved into my street. He's always working on his car. He's eighteen, nineteen maybe. He's got this scar down one side of his face. He must have got it in a fight. It looks cool. It makes him look hard, like a gangster. He stares at me as I walk past. I might get chatting to him.

11

The two girls that she usually hung around with were taken aback by this. Only one of them had a boyfriend and he was already at university studying psychology. Ali had enjoyed shocking them. When they asked her about it the next day and the day after that, she decided that she had to have this young man with the scar on his face.

"That's done," Stephen said. "Shall we go?"

He tucked his sunglasses into the neck of his polo shirt. The light glinted off the lenses and his fingers played around the frame as if to check that they were sitting at the right angle. It irked her and she had an urge to ruffle them so that they were crooked. Out of the corner of her eye, she noticed Hannah emerging from the women's toilets.

"At last!" Jackson said, under his breath.

"I'm coming, I'm coming," Hannah called, making a little run towards them, her breasts bouncing up and down in her tight T-shirt. Her lips were scarlet and her hair looked bigger, as though she'd upended her head under the hand dryer in the toilets. Ali ran her fingers through her own hair, flat and plain. Maybe she should have washed it, made more of an effort.

A couple of lads who were sitting in the McDonald's seats stared at Hannah and said something out loud. Hannah turned briefly and flashed them a shaky smile. Ali didn't catch what had been said, but Jackson stiffened.

"What did he say?" he said when she reached them.

"Nothing," Hannah said.

"He said something. What did he say?"

"It wasn't important!"

"Then just tell me," Jackson said, looking crossly at Hannah and then turning to the boys sitting in McDonald's.

"Just – you know – stuff about how I looked," Hannah said.

Without another word Jackson walked forward, towards where the boys were sitting.

Stephen swore.

"Why doesn't he just ignore it?" Hannah said.

"What did he say?" Ali said.

"Nothing, just some stupid comment. That's why I smiled to show them I didn't care. I just wish Jackson would lighten up."

The lads were standing up and Jackson was arguing with them. Jackson's voice was louder than theirs and he seemed to be getting angrier. One of the boys had his arm in the air, his finger pointing towards Jackson. The other was looking sheepish, as though he hadn't expected trouble. There was a barrier between them sectioning off the McDonald's tables and Jackson was leaning across it, swearing at them, gesticulating with his arm.

Suddenly the lad who was pointing his finger grabbed Jackson's shirt and pulled it. Jackson made to scramble across the barrier. Chairs got knocked over and a table pushed back. Some people stood up from their tables and backed off.

"Oh no," Hannah said.

In a second Stephen was there, sidestepping the barrier, holding the two apart, the other lad pulling his friend back.

"Back off!" Stephen said, his voice loud and commanding.

He was taller than the two lads and both of them seemed to notice his scar at the same moment and stepped back. The one who'd been pointing his finger was speaking low, spitting out

13

words. Jackson was still leaning forward, being held in place by Stephen's arm.

"I didn't mean no trouble, mate..."

"Just having a laugh. Didn't know she was your bird..."

"Keep your shirt on. No offence intended."

Jackson turned away. His face was red and he was staring at the ground. Stephen followed him, putting his hand on his arm, but Jackson shook it off and said something to him. Stephen looked exasperated.

"It's not my fault!" Hannah said, when the four of them were outside walking towards the car.

"I never said it was your fault," Jackson said, brushing his T-shirt down.

Stephen had put his sunglasses on and was quiet. Ali looked at Jackson. His shoulders were squared and he kept turning to look back at the services as if someone might be following him.

"You all right?" Ali said.

He nodded, stiffly.

Inside the car Hannah sat as close to the window as possible. Jackson was looking out the other side. Stephen gave Ali a look of forbearance.

"So are we going up to Blackwood Park?" he said, trying to sound cheerful.

"I'm not bothered," Hannah said.

"Let's go," Jackson said. "I could do with the fresh air. This place stinks of petrol."

"Blackwood Park it is," Stephen said.

THREE

They got to Blackwood just after nine.

Stephen left his car in one of the roads that snaked round the perimeter. They began to walk up the path to the sports area where most of the kids hung out. It was dark and there were lights along the way but they were spaced out. The rest of the park was a swathe of black, the street lights tiny in the distance.

Ali zipped up her sweatshirt. It had been a warm May day but now it felt chilly, more like autumn than spring.

It was an open park with no fence or gates. It had a lake down one end and woods further on. At the end nearest to Ali's school there was a sports centre and a scrubby area of the park where the changing rooms had once been. It was open yet quite private. The huts were boarded up and padlocked, but there were old benches for resting on and picnic tables to sit at. The area was divided off from the tennis courts and five-a-side pitches by a thick fringe of trees and bushes. When it got dark some of the glow from the floodlights washed across them. It was a place they and other kids from their school spent time at, if the weather was good. Nobody bothered them, and it was nicer than sitting in the garden of some pub worrying about whether they'd be thrown out for being underage.

The previous summer there were nights when twenty or

more kids were up there. On other nights there might just be a handful. When it was late and the floodlights went off, the place plunged into darkness. Sometimes kids brought candles, but mostly they just sat in the dark, their eyes adjusting to the blackness. Later, they stumbled home along the pathway, lighting their way down the track with cigarette lighters and the glow of mobile phones.

Ali walked along behind Jackson and Hannah. Since they'd got out of the car, neither of them had said a word to each other. She looked back. Stephen was carrying a cooler box with cans of beer in it. The sight of it irked her. Everyone else just carried the beers in their hands, but Stephen insisted on the cooler box. It was as if they were out on a family picnic.

For eight weeks they'd been a couple. Her mum hadn't approved of him at all. *He's a tearaway. He has a police record for carrying a knife. He has a temper and almost ended up in prison. And he drives that car too fast.* But these had been the things that had attracted her to Stephen. He seemed like a bad boy. A character from a film or book. It made him dangerous to know. He could be her older boyfriend with a dramatic past. The scar on his face was evidence of this past. She'd imagined herself jumping into the passenger seat of his car as the engine was revving up. Then the two of them would speed away as though they were fugitives.

Driving around with Stephen hadn't turned out quite as she'd expected. Mostly he sat silently concentrating on the road, and they seemed to follow the same circuits every time they went out. Along the A13, up to the Queen Elizabeth Bridge, around the Purfleet docks, cutting across country up to Brentwood and

Hornchurch. Then they'd go back on to the dual carriageway for the ride home, towards the big Ford factory, and pull in opposite at Harry's Diner. There they would sit in the car for an hour or so kissing and touching.

After a few weeks she was bored. She was on the brink of dumping him when her mum had a quiet word with her, telling her that she and her dad thought that Stephen was too old for her. They wanted her to give him up, concentrate on her studies. She was aiming for Cambridge, after all.

She couldn't end it with him then.

One day, when he was picking her up from school, a couple of other kids from her class, Hannah Cunningham and Ryan Jackson, were hanging around. When Stephen's car pulled up, Jackson walked across to it and nodded admiringly.

"This is my boyfriend's car," she'd said.

Stephen got out then and started to talk to Jackson.

"It's a GTI Turbo," he said. "I got it at the auctions."

"Nice, Ali," Hannah said.

"What, the car or the boyfriend?" Ali said.

"Want to come for a ride?" Stephen said.

They got in and drove around for a couple of hours. Afterwards Stephen said, "I liked your friends. Ask them if they want to come out on Sunday." She'd felt awkward. They weren't exactly her *friends*. They were just kids she knew. She asked them anyway and they'd seemed pleased.

They went out as a foursome a couple of times a week and headed for places. Southend or Cambridge or Stansted Airport. Mostly it was just a round trip, but they'd usually stop at a services. She had to admit that Hannah and Jackson brightened things up. The three of them talked while Stephen drove. She was happier. Everyone seemed happy for a while.

Now they all seemed fed up. Hannah and Jackson falling out over the smallest thing. Stephen and her idling along like a married couple.

If only he hadn't brought the cool box; if only he stopped going on about Jonesy or his car or speed cameras; if only he kept his sunglasses off until he got out into the sunshine. If only he were a *different person*.

When they got past the tennis courts and through the trees, they found about ten kids sitting there. On one of the tables were some tea lights in small glass saucers that someone had brought. They were all wearing jumpers and a couple of the girls looked cold. But they were chatting and laughing. Some were smoking cigarettes and others were passing round some dope. They nodded and raised a hand in greeting to the four of them.

Ali followed Hannah and Jackson to a table where some other kids were sitting. Stephen put the cooler box on the grass and got the beers out. Then he walked a few paces and picked up a plastic crate and sat on it and opened his can of beer. He stared off into the distance as if he didn't want to be there. She looked into the cool box. She could see the blue ice packs that kept the beers cold. Her mum had them in the freezer cabinet. Her gran probably had them. When she lifted her eyes, she saw Jackson looking down at them. His forehead crinkled. He glanced up then and caught her eye. He made a face and she had to stop herself from grinning wildly. Everyone else had travelled light, but Stephen had his cool box and freezer packs.

Again she and Jackson were thinking about the same thing.

The sound of Hannah's voice cut across her thoughts.

"Why are you so jealous?" she said to Jackson. "Why did you have to go and start a fight? It made me look stupid."

Jackson didn't answer. His previous relaxed expression changed.

"Well?" Hannah said, her voice strident.

"I'm not jealous."

"Why'd you do it, then?"

Ali turned away from them. Their argument continued and she tried not to listen. Stephen was staring into the darkness. The faint light from the floodlights lit up the side of his face and she could see the scar. It was raised and pink: skin that had been broken, the line of the join puckered and shiny. Stephen had told her that a boy with a point to prove had cut his face with a kitchen knife. He had been sentenced to twenty-four months in Young Offender's Institution.

"Just shut up! Shut up! I'm not jealous. I couldn't care less if you want to flash your tits at other blokes, I couldn't care less!"

Jackson got up suddenly and inadvertently kicked the cool box over. Stephen looked at him.

"Sorry, mate," he said angrily, and walked off towards the trees.

Some of the other kids glanced over, the noise of their chatter stopping for a few moments. Then it started again. Stephen huffed and reached over to right the box. Hannah sat with her arms crossed and seemed as if she was on the brink of crying. Ali looked after Jackson, but he had disappeared into the trees.

She sighed. Could tonight get any worse?

"I'll go and talk to him," she said.

No one said anything.

The trees that bordered the playing courts were old and gnarled and looked like they'd been there for years before the sports centre had even been built. Sometimes, during the day, when it was possible to see from tree to tree, kids hung ropes from the branches and made rudimentary swings. At night the space was velvety dark, the branches and leaves blocking out the glow from the floodlights and the courts beyond. Walking in, past the first line of trees, Ali was struck by the stillness and quiet, as though she'd closed a door behind her and shut out all the other kids who were socializing on the grass.

She saw Jackson leaning against a tree trunk. She walked up to him.

"Hi," she said.

"Did she send you?" he said.

She shook her head. "Why did you get upset at those boys? Are you worried that she's going to go off with someone?"

"No," he said. "She doesn't get it. I'm not jealous of her. She wants to go off with someone, that's all right with me. It's not exactly going to *break my heart*..."

"I don't get it."

"Those kids in the service station? They were insulting *me*. Not her."

Ali frowned. She didn't understand what he meant.

A sound came from somewhere, further in the trees. It distracted her and she looked around.

"What was that?"

"Dunno," Jackson said. "Where did it come from?"

"Over there, I think," she whispered, pointing.

"Someone's spying on us! Maybe it's some young kids."

Jackson stepped sideways, staring into the darkness. He moved forward a few paces. Ali followed. He was looking upwards.

"What?" she said, confused.

"There's someone in that tree, look," Jackson said, relaxed again, pointing to a tree further along, closer to the playing courts.

She looked upwards. It took a moment but she could see a shape. Someone had climbed up into a tree.

"Hey!" Jackson called out.

He went a couple of steps further. Ali could see the figure more clearly now. She thought it was a man, sitting on one of the big branches.

"What you doing, mate?" Jackson called.

Under his breath he said, "Me Tarzan you Jane" and Ali smiled. The figure didn't move. Was it someone? Or were they imagining things, seeing shapes or shadows and thinking it was a person?

"Leave it," Ali said dismissively, "it's nothing. Come back and sort it out with Hannah..."

There was a sudden movement and the person jumped from the branch. Ali watched with surprise. She saw him coming down, his body dropping. It happened in the blink of an eye. He was there then he wasn't. The branch gave off a loud creak and then seemed to spring back up again.

Jackson swore and moved forward.

She saw a face then. A young man. He wasn't on ground level; he was still up in the tree. He had jumped, but hadn't

21

landed on the ground. She could only see his knees. They swung to and fro. His shoes dangled loosely.

"Oh no," Ali said, the words squeaking out of her.

The young man was *hanging* from the branch.

Jackson moved swiftly forward and lunged at the flailing legs as if he was doing some kind of rugby tackle.

What was he doing?

Jackson was *hugging* the young man's legs.

No.

He was trying to lift them, struggling as though he had a sack of potatoes in his arms. His head turned slightly and he gasped.

"Get the others. Get an ambulance. . ."

Ali just stared. She looked upwards. Was there a rope there? It was too dark to see into the tree. The face was there, but in the shadows.

"Ali, get help!" Jackson gasped.

She had no understanding of what was happening. She couldn't move. Her breath had gone and her legs felt weak.

"Ali, ALI, ALI!" Jackson shouted.

She turned and ran out of the trees. When she got to the edge she saw everyone sitting in the same place and felt herself sinking into the general murmur of conversation. Hannah had moved to another table and was talking to some kids from school. Stephen had his back to her.

She called out his name. Then she said it louder. Then she screamed.

"STEPHEN!"

He looked round. Everyone looked round.

"HELP, HELP, GET AN AMBULANCE!"

"What's up, what's going on?"

People started to get up. Stephen was by her side. She was crying, trying to speak.

"A man's tried to hang himself from the trees. . ."

She pointed behind. Stephen was the first to go past her, then the others. Then Hannah. Then she followed.

FOUR

A couple of other boys were standing shoulder by shoulder with Jackson, taking the weight of the young man, hoisting him upwards so that the rope that held him to the branch of the tree was slack. Kids held their mobile phones up. One boy had a torch. The dark cave of trees was suddenly speckled with moving lights. The torch moved up and down, pausing on the rope, dropping down to his face, then back up again. Ali's eyes followed it, dazed by what she was seeing.

"It's Feeny!" someone said.

"Daniel Feeny!"

The young man's face was pale and slack. Every time the torch lit it up, Ali could see who it was. Daniel Feeny, a boy from their class, not a young man at all.

"What's he doing?"

"What a nutter!"

"Poor Daniel."

"I can't believe it! Daniel Feeny."

On the ground it looked like a rugby scrum. The faces of the boys were blank, concentrated, not showing any emotion. Jackson's face was rapt. He was struggling to raise up the inert Daniel Feeny.

"Higher," he puffed, "lift him higher."

Stephen climbed the tree. He shimmied up the trunk and then pulled himself from branch to branch until he got to the one that held the rope. Then he lay along it, his feet touching the trunk, his arm reaching out towards the knotted rope.

"Gimme the light," he shouted, and the beam from the torch zigzagged wildly while Stephen's hand touched the rope, felt over it, scrabbled at it, pulled at it.

An ambulance had been called. It would take time. Ten minutes, someone said. Ten long minutes. Ali was standing shoulder to shoulder with Hannah. They were a couple of strides away from the platform of boys holding Daniel Feeny's body up. Some of the other girls were behind them. Hannah's hand was clutching Ali's forearm, her long nails digging into Ali's skin.

"We just saw him drop," Ali said, hopelessly, a few kids looking round for a second. "We thought he was jumping off the branch. We didn't even know it was Daniel."

Daniel Feeny was tall and pale with longish hair that he tied back. He never took his blazer off winter or summer. Ali hardly knew him. He was one of the quiet kids; always had his head in a book or a magazine. She remembered that he'd been bullied in the past but lately she hadn't heard of anything. He was someone she never had any time for.

Now his face was ghastly. He looked half dead.

"I need a knife," Stephen shouted, his voice full of authority.

Another lad stretched up the tree trunk and held out what looked like a flick knife, but it was too far for Stephen to reach.

"Throw it up," Stephen shouted. "Come on, throw the knife up!"

The lad went to throw and then shook his head. The light

wasn't bright enough for him to get an aim. Other kids went over and hoisted him up on to the lower branch of the tree.

Hannah was swearing softly under her breath. Ali's arm was hurting from her tight clasp. The lad passed the knife up to Stephen. Then it looked as though Stephen was hugging the branch, reaching as far forward as he could. With one hand he held the slackened rope. With the other he began to saw at it, his elbow moving back and forward.

"It's coming," he shouted after a few moments.

Everyone stopped talking. There wasn't a sound.

"It's nearly there," Stephen said, grunting.

From somewhere far behind, Ali could hear a siren. There it was, down at the bottom of the park, making its way slowly up the incline.

"It's almost..." Stephen said, puffing.

Everyone surged forward. Hannah was there, just beside Jackson. Ali was on the other side, looking up at the hanging boy. Beyond him she could see Stephen's face, his teeth bared, his eyes fearful.

Then the rope broke and Daniel Feeny slumped down, his top half falling forward, caught by all of them.

"Watch it..."

"Steady now..."

"Watch his head..."

"Careful..."

"Lay him on his side..."

"Easy does it..."

They carried him a few steps and then lowered him on to the grass.

26

"The rope!" someone said.

Jackson put his arms out, pushing people away. "Move back. Give us some room. Someone shine the torch on his neck."

The circle of bright light picked out the rope around Daniel's neck. There was a gasp. The sight of it was shocking. A crude piece of rope digging into the skin. Jackson knelt down. He put his fingers on the rope, pulling it gently at the front, trying to loosen it. Hannah was beside him.

"Put him in the recovery position, on his side, let me..." she said.

"Is he still breathing?" Ali whispered.

Hannah rolled Daniel on to his side, lifting one knee forward.

"Is he alive?" someone shouted.

"I don't know," Jackson said.

"Get a mirror. Someone get a mirror," Stephen said.

His voice was loud, commanding. He'd got down from the tree and was standing looking at the boy on the ground. Hannah dashed off. Stephen took her place. He looked at the rope around Daniel's neck.

"Careful. You don't want to restrict his breathing any further. We need a mirror! Someone must have a mirror."

Hannah appeared suddenly with her candy-striped bag. She was rummaging about in it. She pulled out a small mirror and held it out to Stephen.

The siren was coming closer. Ali could hear it. A few of the kids had left the wood and gone back out to the clearing to direct the paramedics.

"Just hold the mirror in front of his mouth. Hold it for a minute. Then see if it's steamed up. See if he's got any breath."

It went silent. Hannah was standing next to Ali, her big bag over her arm. Nobody moved. Nobody said a word. Everyone was still and tense. From behind, there was the sound of loud voices.

Jackson held the mirror to Daniel Feeny's mouth. Then he raised it and his face broke into a smile.

"He's breathing," he said.

Everyone smiled uneasily.

"He's alive," Stephen said, his voice calm. "He's still alive."

The paramedics carried Daniel Feeny to the ambulance. He was flat out on a stretcher. He was covered in a sheet of foil. He had a brace around his neck and shoulders and only a small square of his face could be seen. His eyes were open but he looked dazed, as if he'd been in a road accident. One of the paramedics was talking to him. "You're all right now, Daniel. We'll look after you now."

The police arrived. Some of the boys swore when they saw them and slipped away. The police were taking names and addresses and a WPC was talking in a soothing voice to a group of girls, one of whom was crying. Jackson and Hannah were sitting on a bench. Hannah was holding the tiny mirror in her hand. Jackson had his arm around her. He looked up at Ali, his eyes holding hers for a second. They had been there when a boy tried to kill himself. Just the two of them. It gave her an odd feeling and she wished for a moment she could say something to him about it.

She walked over to Stephen, who was talking to a policeman. He had his hands held out, explaining what had happened. His voice was full of excitement. He looked flushed and more alive than he had all evening. She put her hand on his arm. It felt rigid.

"It was my girlfriend who first saw him. She was the one who called out for help."

"You've done a good job, son. All of you," the policeman said. "You've just saved someone's life."

When the policeman walked off, Stephen turned to look at her. His eyes were glassy, as if he was close to tears. She squeezed his hand.

FIVE

Stephen drove away from Blackwood Park. He sped along the road as if he were making a quick escape. Jackson and Hannah hadn't wanted to come. They were sitting talking quietly with some other kids, but Stephen was keen to get away. Ali had been disappointed but went along anyway. All the way down from the park he held her hand tightly and once in the car he kissed her hard on the mouth and made her insides tingle.

He drove silently.

Ali's stomach felt light. Daniel Feeny had tried to commit *suicide*. She and Jackson had seen him up the tree. Stephen had climbed up and cut the rope. Hannah had made sure he was in the recovery position and produced a mirror to check for signs of life. There had been other kids there, she knew that, but it seemed, in her head, as though the four of them had been on their own.

Suicide.

He had wanted to *die*.

The word gave her a heavy feeling.

There was traffic around, but the road wasn't busy. Stephen was sitting straight, his spine flat against the seat. His hands were stretched out, holding the steering wheel. He looked like he was clinging to it. After a while they went on to the A13 and drove at speed along the dual carriageway.

She'd seen Daniel Feeny during the week at school. Hadn't she? He was in her form group, came to some of her classes, used the refectory, the library. She tried to think hard but she couldn't quite remember him or picture him anywhere. Had he been in school that week?

The bullying that Daniel Feeny had experienced had been years before, she was sure. The boys involved had been punished and they'd stopped. Or maybe they'd just turned their sights on someone else. She hadn't heard of Daniel Feeny having any problems lately. But then, Daniel Feeny wasn't someone who ever *registered* with her. He was just an odd kid in the class. Not involved in any particular group of friends. Not someone she would have exchanged half a dozen words with.

To attempt *suicide*. How low must he have been?

She noticed the car was slowing. In the distance she could see the lights of the giant Ford car plant, and opposite, on their side of the dual carriageway, the tall post with the flickering pink-neon light that said *Harry's Diner*.

She sighed quietly. Whenever she and Stephen were alone, they always seemed to end up at this place. They never came here when Hannah and Jackson were with them. It had to be just the two of them. She'd asked him once why they didn't park up in the forest or in a street. He told her that he liked the absolute privacy and the sound of the traffic passing.

The car was slowing down, coming up to the slip road for the café. Behind it was the old Ford car sales depot. The whole area was as big as a football field. Stephen had told her that it had once held a car showroom and car-repair shop and a petrol station. It had long been closed down and someone had put a café there, right at the front, close to the road. The café had a name that made it sound like a glossy American restaurant but it was only a single-storey building the size of a mobile home.

Tonight, because it was the weekend, the café was closed.

Stephen drove slowly past it, on to the old car park behind where they usually parked up after buying a drink or chips. Tonight they had nothing.

"Wish that café was still open," she said, in a low voice.

"Mmm," Stephen said. "Have a beer."

Ali looked behind. In the floor space behind the driver's seat was the cool box. She leaned across and pulled a can out.

"Want one?" she said.

He shook his head.

"Still cold," she said, blowing gently through her teeth, remembering Jackson's look when they'd both seen the freezer blocks.

The car went slowly through the open ground behind the café, moving further away from the road. Stephen steered between the concrete foundations of the car sales showroom on one side and the disused petrol pumps and the derelict kiosk on the other. He was heading towards the very back of the car park. The car dipped and rose over the uneven ground.

"I need some air," Stephen said.

They came to stop seconds later and he flung his door open and got out, half walking, half running towards an old lorry container that sat up against some wire fence at the back of the parking area.

Ali watched him go. She thought he might need to pee. He disappeared round the back of the container. She waited for a while, aware that she was on her own in a car in the middle of a piece of derelict land just off the A13. She was miles away from civilization. She wished that Jackson and Hannah were in the back. She drank her beer and felt the bubbles going down her throat. There was cold air coming in through Stephen's door, so she leaned across and pulled it shut.

Daniel Feeny would be in hospital. She pictured him being carried into A & E by the paramedics as nurses rushed to see what they could do. How would he feel? Would he be shocked? Or just sad that he hadn't succeeded? Maybe he had wanted to be stopped. Possibly he had actually waited for someone to come into the tree area before he jumped? She felt herself on the edge of a shiver. She didn't want to think about it any more.

She wondered what the others were doing. She gave a small smile. She had a good idea. Over the past weeks, during long drives home late at night, they'd spent a lot of time snogging in the back seat and once or twice she'd known that they were up to much more. Mostly she'd just closed her eyes and leaned her head on the passenger window.

For all their arguing, Jackson and Hannah were very physical. A few hours ago, at the motorway service station, they had fallen out, but now they were close again. No doubt at that very moment they were in Jackson's bedroom lying on his double bed wrestling slowly with each other. That was what it was like with them. One minute they were quarrelling, the next they were in a clinch. How different to her and Stephen. They never seemed to fall out. They just jogged along together. Stephen was hard to argue with. He simply didn't rise to disagreements. Sometimes he seemed downright cold. And when it came to them being physical, he was just the same. They drove miles to sit in this odd deserted place and yet all they ever did was kiss and touch.

The only thing Stephen was passionate about was his car.

She suddenly wondered where he was. She felt a flicker of worry about him. They were *all* upset about what had happened, but he'd seemed rattled; overexcited when talking to the police, morose when driving.

He'd been gone too long. She got out of the car and zipped up her top and pulled the collar up. The headlights of the car were still on, so she could steer clear of the scattered debris of upended supermarket trolleys, crates, black plastic rubbish bags and Amazonian weeds that had forced their way through the concrete and tarmac. The car park was quiet, but every now and then the traffic from the A13 could be heard: a lorry trundling along, a car zipping past, a motorbike speeding along, leaving the buzzing sound of its exhaust in its wake.

She called out Stephen's name and heard a retching sound. She stepped gingerly round the edge of the old container and saw him leaning up against the side, his head bent over.

He'd been sick.

"Are you all right?" she said.

He nodded and stood up straight. In his hand he had a white handkerchief. It was too dark here to see his face properly. He stepped towards her and she put her hand on his arm and felt it trembling.

"I thought that boy was going to die."

"He didn't, though," she said rubbing his arm.

He felt cold. She took one of his hands between both of hers.

"When I was on that branch, when I was trying to cut that rope, I thought, *It's too late, he's choked already. We've not been quick enough.*"

"But we were," she said, softly.

He held the handkerchief up to his mouth. Then he raised it to his eyes. She looked at him with dismay. Was he crying?

"Don't be upset," she said.

"I'm all right," he said. He blew his nose loudly and then shoved the handkerchief back into his pocket.

"We did a good thing," she said.

Stephen nodded. She leaned her back against the container, feeling the crumbling of loose paint and rust. Stephen stood in front of her. Close up she could see his face. He looked stricken, a faraway look in his eyes.

"Shame Harry's is closed. Could really do with some chips now," she said, trying to lighten the mood.

Stephen gave a half smile. "Don't tell the others, will you. About me. . ."

She shook her head. He looked different. His clothes were dirty from climbing the tree, his top covered in grubby marks. She felt a spurt of affection for him. She stepped forward and put her arms around him. He hugged her back. They walked out and round the front of the old container.

"What's this made out of? Cast iron?" Ali said, stepping across and running her nails along the grooves, making a tapping noise.

"It's an old ship container," Stephen said. "Lorries carry them to and from the docks. Someone's dumped it here."

Ali walked the length of it. At the other end the door was hanging open and there was a pair of black leather boots standing at the entrance, as if someone had taken them off and walked inside.

"Has someone been *living* here?" she said.

"Maybe," Stephen said. "I was here in the winter a few times. Once I saw a couple of men coming out of here. They looked like homeless types and it was pretty cold."

Ali put her head inside the cabin. It was pitch-dark. She kicked the shoes out of the way and walked back to Stephen.

"Let's go home before I freeze to death," she said.

They walked towards the car. The atmosphere was lighter. Ali put her hand on Stephen's arm and it felt soft, pliable.

"What a night," Stephen said, driving off.

The night we saved someone's life, Ali thought, closing her eyes.

SIX

Year Thirteen

"Jackson wants to see us," Alison said.

"So?" Stephen said.

They were standing outside the building society where Stephen worked. He was holding a cigarette between his thumb and his forefinger. He inhaled and then held it close to his lips while he exhaled. There were a couple of other people smoking on the same bit of pavement.

"You smoking?" she said.

"What do you want, Ali?" he said.

"Jackson asked me to tell you. I'm just passing the message on."

Stephen was wearing a silver-grey suit and dark pink shirt. Round his neck was bright red tape which held an identity card. He'd tucked it under his tie but she could still see the company logo above his photograph. She twiddled with the card hanging round her own neck. She read the words *East London Sixth Form College* upside down. Her picture was underneath. A head and shoulders shot. Like something you might see on a police record.

"What does he want?" Stephen said, after a few moments.

He was staring across the road, his eyes fixed on something. He hadn't looked straight at her, hadn't made any eye contact. She sighed.

"I don't know. He says he's been working. As a waiter in a bar."

"Why come back now?"

"I don't know. That's why he wants to meet us. You and me. He says he won't talk about it unless we're both there."

"It's obvious what it's going to be about. I thought we agreed that we wouldn't talk about Feeny again."

"I know," she said.

"What's the point of dragging it up?"

"He says he just wants to meet. Just once, that's all. He says he hasn't got long."

"What, is he rushing off back to Brighton?"

"He wants to meet at the sports centre café. Seven o'clock, tonight."

"I don't need to go over all this stuff from the past," he said, taking a long pull from the cigarette and holding his breath before blowing the smoke out and chucking the butt into the road.

"Will you come?" she said.

"Maybe," he said, the breeze ruffling his tie.

She watched as he walked back into the building society. Through the glass she could see him go up to a young woman at the reception area. The young woman said something to him and looked out in Alison's direction. Stephen replied and the young woman smiled and nodded her head.

Alison walked away, across the high street, towards the bus stop.

At home she made some pasta. She took her time cutting up the vegetables. She browned the meat and added the sauce. Then she left it to simmer for forty minutes. She picked up the timer clock and set it so that she didn't forget the time.

Her dad was sitting in the dining room. His laptop was open in front of him. As she passed she saw that he was working on a spreadsheet.

"Busy?" she said.

"Got a new contract with a haulage company from Finland," he said, turning round briefly, then back to the screen. "Trying to work out a schedule so that we can unload their ships without creating a backlog to our regular customers."

"Great to have a dad with such an interesting job, yawn, yawn," her mum said, coming into the room.

"Huh! Unlike yours!" her dad said, in a sing-song voice. "*Oh, Mrs Martin's got bowel problems and must see the doctor; old Mr Jennings needs his flu injection. . .*"

"At least I'm dealing with *people*. Not cargo. Not rubber tyres from China or bags of cement from Russia."

"Enough!" Alison said, a smile on her face.

"Who's got the best job, Ali?" her dad said.

"Go on, Ali, you tell him. Who's got the most *important* job?"

"Who wants pasta and mince, otherwise known as spag

bol?" Alison said, leaving them, walking back out to the kitchen.

The timer still had twenty minutes to run. She looked at the clock on the wall. It was ten to six. She'd serve the food up. Maybe she'd even try and eat some. Then she would get ready to go and meet Jackson and Stephen at the sports centre.

"Are you all right, love?" her mum said, coming into the kitchen.

"Yes," she said.

"Only I heard you in the middle of the night. Moving about."

"Insomnia."

"The exams?"

"Yes. You know how important it is that I get my grades."

"I know that, love, but you know it's not the end of the world if you don't get into Downing College."

"It is to me," she said.

Everything she'd done in the last two years had been leading to this, to these exams, to this university place.

"It's going to be very odd. You not living here. I know it was what me and Dad wanted, but if you changed your mind and decided to go to one of the London universities, we'd still be glad," her mum said, taking the lid off the pot and looking in. "I hate the idea of you living in Cambridge. On your own, in a strange place."

Alison didn't answer. She reached out and stroked her mum's arm. She didn't understand. That was exactly why

Alison wanted to go to Cambridge. To be somewhere strange, where no one knew her.

She was the first one at the café.

The small cafeteria had been built into the corner of the sports centre. It had started as a wall of machines serving cold and hot drinks, and sweets and snacks. The healthy-food drive had changed all that. Now it had tables and a counter and it sold fruit and soups and salads. Kids had to go outside the park to the nearby shops to buy their Cokes and chocolate, but then, the cafeteria had never been designed for them. It was mainly for the paying customers of the gym.

The only time they had used it was in the days after Daniel Feeny's attempted suicide. The local newspaper had wanted them there for an interview and photographs. They'd all turned up early and been excited. Even Stephen had looked pleased with himself.

While she waited for the others, Alison bought a drink and sat down on a seat by the window. She kept her eye on the car park outside. She wondered if Stephen would drive. She had no idea whether he still had a car. He'd moved out of his parents' house and was now living in a flat near the high street. Jackson would walk from his parents' house. It was five minutes away.

That day, when the press wanted to interview them, they'd all met at Jackson's house and come together. Hannah had brought a hair dryer and insisted on making them all look good. She'd also got her make-up bag out to cover blemishes. The boys had laughed and refused point-blank. It meant that Hannah only had Alison to work on. The four of them had walked up the path to the sports centre like some girl–boy band, looking pleased with themselves.

"How does it feel," the reporter asked, "to have saved someone's life?"

Even the photographer joined in. "When you saved the boy's life, how did you feel?"

They'd all smiled and laughed and joked and said it was nothing. It wasn't just them, they'd said; there'd been loads of other kids there that night.

"But how did it feel, deep inside?"

They'd had to pose and smile. Each couple had to kiss and hug. Jackson had his arms around Hannah and Stephen had held her proudly, possessively, beaming with a smile. Then the four of them had to stand in a line. The camera clicked, and they all felt important.

Now Alison's eye was drawn to a silver car coming into the car park. It turned into a parking space. Stephen got out of the silver car and just then, as if by magic, Jackson appeared at the top of the lane.

Now just three of them were together again.

How special they had felt, two years ago. *How did it feel to save a boy's life?* They'd been asked over and over. It felt good. It felt wonderful. It felt like there was a point to being alive.

To save Daniel's life. It was the most astonishing thing.

So why, five weeks later, after trying to be his friend, after trying to help him, did they end up killing him?

SEVEN
Year Eleven

After the newspaper report, the three of them, Ali, Jackson and Hannah, became celebrities in school. The teachers, the dinner staff, the caretakers, the office workers all gave reassuring nods and pats on the shoulder when they passed. In class, many pupils wanted a run-down on what happened and the lesson paused while Ali or Hannah or Jackson related it again. There were always masses of questions.

"Who was the fourth boy? The one who cut the rope?"

"When did you first notice Feeny? Did you think he was dead?"

"Did you give him mouth to mouth?"

"Was he breathing?"

"How come he didn't break his neck?"

Eventually the teacher said "Enough! Enough!" and the lesson went on.

The head of year, Mrs Caine, called each of them into her office for a chat. When it was Ali's turn, she told the story in a shortened version.

"Jackson and I saw him jump. Jackson realized that he hadn't reached the ground, so he rushed forward and grabbed his legs, trying to hold him up. . ."

"So that the rope wasn't taking Daniel's weight."

"We didn't know it was Daniel at that point. It was dark. . ."

"It was very quick thinking. If you hadn't been there, Daniel Feeny would most certainly have died."

"Then Stephen, my boyfriend, climbed the tree and cut the rope with a knife."

"It must have been shocking for all of you."

"Hannah put him in the recovery position. Jackson put a mirror to his lips and we saw that he was still alive. There were loads of other kids there and they helped. I feel a bit of a fraud being called a hero."

"Well, thank goodness you were there," Mrs Caine said. "Now you have to put it all behind you and get on with the exams. The first one is English? On Thursday? Good luck with that."

"Thanks, miss."

"Remember, Alison, statistically speaking, fewer students from this area go to university than almost any other place in England. And hardly any go to Oxford or Cambridge. That's why we're focusing on three or four students who could get those top grades. We think you're one of them."

"I know, miss."

Later, after doing test papers in history, she thought of her chat with Mrs Caine and felt an uncomfortable feeling of pressure. It was something she hadn't thought about for a while. Ever since year ten, she'd been having personal mentoring sessions with her head of year. Getting ready for university. She'd gone along with it. One of the girls she hung around with had also had similar sessions. Her mum and dad had been thrilled. But it was a long way off, and it hadn't interfered with the rest of her life, so she hadn't minded. Now, amid the excitement of recent events, the pressure, the expectation, the assumption of her *going* was building up. Did she want to go to Cambridge? Did she even want to go to university? Sometimes she wondered if all this stuff had been a trigger for her getting together with Stephen Grainger. To let people know that she wasn't simply on a conveyor belt.

She wished she could talk to Jackson about this stuff. His plans for university were clear and solid. But every time she saw him, Hannah was there. She had her arm draped around his neck or her hand linked through his.

She tried to talk about it to Stephen when they were alone, in the dark of the car, parked in the yard behind Harry's Diner. But Stephen just murmured agreement with her. There was a lot of fervent kissing and Stephen seemed to get excited quickly. It was as if the hero bit had fired him up. He undid her buttons swiftly. He pushed aside her skirt. Things became heated and Ali ended up feeling dazed and exhausted.

She continued revising for her exams. At the same time, she and Hannah and Jackson basked in everyone's admiration. And Stephen had some extra publicity. A reporter had found out about his past, the trouble he had been in at school and with the police. He found a photo which showed Stephen's scar and used it alongside an article about him. BAD BOY DOES GOOD. Stephen had been embarrassed reading it. He'd shrugged it off, made a joke about it. Later, though, Ali had found it torn out of the paper and folded in four in his glove compartment.

Stephen was pleased with himself. He seemed to have a constant smile on his face. He said that Jonesy, his old teacher from school, was proud of him. There was talk about Stephen going with Jonesy to the Isle of Man stock car races in August.

Somehow they had travelled back in time. On the night of the suicide attempt the foursome was fractured, close to being broken. Then, bathing in their success, they were together again. Stephen and Ali; Jackson and Hannah. The kids who saved a boy's life.

The GCSE exams wents by, one after another. Ali followed her timetable of revision. She stayed up late practising timed essays and spent a lot of time on revision websites. Her room had little islands of books and papers dotted around the carpet: history paper one, paper two; English literature; English language; maths one; maths two. There was hardly room to walk from her bed to her wardrobe. She got to each exam early with her special pencil case and her bottle of water and her packet of mints. She queued up with the others in the playground or in the well of the hall while the tables were being made ready. While she was in the middle of a paper she'd look up and see Hannah's head a few places in front and Jackson's profile a couple of aisles away. She ticked the exams off one by one, filing away the books and papers for each subject until all that was left fitted on her desk. The carpet in her room was clear except for the usual clutter of socks and trainers and jeans that had collapsed in on themselves.

Mrs Caine called all three of them to see her. Ali had just finished the second GCSE sociology paper. When she walked along the corridor, Hannah was already there, sitting outside the head of year's office.

"Hi," Hannah said. "You finished?"

Ali shook her head. "I've got paper two history next week and drama. You?"

"Art, next week. Three papers. Then ICT."

It felt odd sitting in the corridor, the two of them, on their own. It was at times like this that Ali was acutely aware that she and Hannah had never been *friends*. The ride in the car weeks before had started a kind of loose bond centred on being a foursome. But she and Hannah had never gravitated towards each other in the past five years, even though they'd been in the same class, day in, day out. They were too different. Hannah wasn't interested in schoolwork. Hannah was leaving school to go and work in her mum's hairdressing shop. Ali was well known as a "boffin" and she was heading for Cambridge.

None of that seemed to matter when they were a foursome but here, in the corridor, waiting to see Mrs Caine, Ali struggled to think of something to say. After a moment, Hannah spoke.

"Seeing Stephen tonight?"

"Probably," she said.

"Can't believe it's been nearly two weeks since that night up Blackwood," Hannah said.

She nodded.

"I keep thinking about Daniel Feeny hanging from that tree," Hannah went on. "What do you think made him do it?"

Ali shrugged her shoulders.

"Some people say that suicide is a cry for help," Hannah said.

Along the corridor, Ali could see Jackson coming. He looked happy. He seemed to be bouncing along. In one hand he was holding his rucksack; in the other he had a badminton racquet. The straps of his rucksack were dragging along the floor.

"All right?" he said as he got closer.

"You're late," Hannah said.

Mrs Caine opened her door at that moment.

"Come in!" she said, more as an instruction than an invitation.

They filed in.

"Sit down, please."

They sat in the soft chairs around the desk, Hannah tucking her big bag under the seat, Jackson looking for somewhere to put his racquet.

"I haven't got long," Mrs Caine said, pulling a letter out of a file. "Mr Feeny, Daniel's father, has sent me this and asked me to read it to you.

"*To the students Hannah, Alison and Ryan,*

"*I wish to give my thanks to you for saving my son's life. You will never know how eternally grateful I am. For this reason, I am making a donation to the school fund of one thousand pounds. It's not a price I would put on my son's life. No amount of money can buy that. It's just a token of thanks. If any of you feel like coming round to see us, you would be very welcome. Please pass on my thanks to the other boy, Stephen.*

"*Yours, Trevor Feeny*

"We are obviously very grateful to Mr Feeny and to all of you. You did a good thing and now the school has been rewarded for it."

Nobody spoke. Hannah fiddled with the handles of her bag.

"Daniel Feeny was badly injured. He has bruising to his larynx, his neck and his shoulders."

"Do they know why he did it?" Hannah asked.

Mrs Caine cleared her throat. It looked as though she didn't want to say.

"It's hardly a secret that Daniel has had some troubles. There are some aggressive elements in this school and I'm afraid Daniel has had experience of this. He has missed a great deal of time during the last two years through absence. It's for this reason that he will not be returning here. In the autumn he will go to a very good school in Essex and re-sit the whole year. I believe his father has plans to relocate."

"That's a shame," Hannah said.

"Yes, it is," Mrs Caine said. "Which is why we had a meeting about Daniel last week, about how to support this move, and we came up with a plan that involved you three."

Ali glanced at Jackson.

"That's if you are willing..."

Jackson sat back, crossing his arms.

"I see that Hannah and Alison, you both live pretty close to Daniel's house. And Ryan just a little bit further. We were hoping that between you, you wouldn't mind dropping off bits of work, handouts, marked essays and so on round to his house."

"I thought he wasn't doing any exams?" Jackson said.

"He's not, but his father is keen that he tries to make up work that he's missed so that he's in a good position for next year."

"Can't this stuff be posted?" Jackson said. "I hardly know the kid."

"It can be posted. Some of it will."

"Or emailed?" Ali added.

"Yes, that too. But we wondered whether you felt, as it was

you three specifically who helped him – and your boyfriend, of course, Alison – we wondered how you felt about being a sort of human link between the school and Daniel himself? If you were to call in and see him a couple of times, bring things from the teachers. Just see how he is."

She looked at each of them.

"He's had a bad time here. . ." she started.

"But, miss, that's not *our* fault," Jackson said. "I know we helped him that night in Blackwood, but we'd have done that for anyone."

Ali found herself nodding.

"Yes, yes. I know what you're telling me, but. . ."

She seemed lost for words. Then she continued.

"Do you not feel, all of you, that what Daniel did, what he tried to do, was a cry for help?"

"That's what I said," Hannah said. "Didn't I? *A cry for help*, I said that."

"Think about where this suicide attempt took place. At the sports centre, near where other students spend time."

"You mean he just wanted attention?" Jackson said.

"Maybe Daniel chose that place because he wanted you, his fellow students, to know what he was going through."

"We did what we could for him."

"Yes, you did. I'm not denying that. But we would hope that this might be a turning point for Daniel. Now, we're not asking you to be best friends, or to even be friends. Just a few friendly faces who call round to give him some school stuff."

Jackson was looking down at his shoes.

"You saved his life two weeks ago. We're just asking you if you might extend a bit of *warmth* in his direction. Just so that when he moves on in September, he has some good memories of this school."

"I'll take some stuff round for him," Hannah said.

"Me too," Ali mumbled.

Jackson didn't say anything.

"That's a good start," Mrs Caine said. "I won't say any more. I'll leave it to you, Ryan. I won't think any worse of you one way or the other."

They left the office and Hannah frowned at Jackson.

"Why do you have to be so negative? It'll only take ten minutes."

"It's nothing to do with me!" he said, with exasperation. "Feeny is not my problem."

Hannah's face hardened. Without a word she walked off, her bag hanging loosely off one shoulder. Jackson stood still. They watched as she reached the end of the corridor and turned out of sight. Jackson said something under his breath.

"She'll be all right," Ali said.

"She's had the hump on and off all day."

"Maybe she's tense about the exams."

"I think she's just tense about me."

Ali didn't answer.

"Why can't I have a nice girlfriend like you, Ali?" he said, throwing his arm around her shoulder, his fingers on the skin of her arm.

She smiled. They walked after Hannah. When they reached the stairs, he pulled his arm away.

"Better go," he said, "got a match."

"Bye."

"See you later," he called.

Then he was gone, his footsteps echoing further down the stairwell. She rubbed her arm at the place where his fingers had touched her skin. *A nice girlfriend like you.* She couldn't help but smile all the way along the corridor.

EIGHT

It was Sunday evening and the four of them were sitting on one of the picnic benches at Blackwood. It was past nine o'clock and the sky was darkening.

"I don't get why you're being so off about this lad, Daniel," Stephen said.

"I'm not being *off*. It's just that I don't want to get involved with him," Jackson said.

Stephen had been to Daniel's Feeny's house that afternoon. His old schoolteacher Jonesy had suggested it and gone along with him. He'd spent a couple of hours talking to Daniel and his dad.

"I quite liked the lad. He seemed friendly enough. He chatted. He's interested in cars and video games. And he hates school. Not much different from most lads of his age."

They were on their own. There were voices from the tennis courts and from further away in the park the sound of male voices shouting; a late football or cricket game in progress. The trees around them were becoming shadowy, losing their individual shapes. The grass was parched and felt dry under Ali's feet. Above them midges were dancing about crazily. Ali had her hands on her neck. She didn't want to get bitten. Stephen was still talking. Ali noticed that he'd begun to touch the scar on his face with one finger, as if feeling to see if it was still there.

Stephen had picked Ali up from her gran's house. She'd spent the afternoon there. She'd mowed the lawn and vacuumed the floors and generally been helpful. Her gran, over eighty, was finding it hard to do stuff for herself. When he called for her, the old lady gave her a powerful squeeze and a ten-pound note.

It was Stephen's decision that they should all meet up at Blackwood to talk about Daniel Feeny. When he first got there, he'd wandered into the tree area and walked up to the very tree from which Daniel had tried to hang himself. Hannah had followed him. It left Jackson and Ali on their own out on the grass – the reverse of the way it had been over two weeks before. Then it had been Jackson and Ali in the trees.

"He nearly died. I think you should give him a chance."

"We know he nearly died. We were *there*," Jackson said.

The four of them had been talking for more than an hour. They talked about that night again. Ali felt déjà vu. As if every comment had been said before, every memory worked and reworked. How many more times were they going to go over it?

"I think Stephen's right. We should help Daniel," Hannah said.

Ali gave a silent sigh.

"You do that if you want. I just don't want to be involved. It happened. We sorted it," Jackson said, staring out into the night, his back to the trees.

"You might actually *like* him," Hannah said.

"I don't want to like him. He's just a kid in my class! I didn't much like him before and unless he's changed. . ."

"Of course he's changed," Stephen said.

"Why?"

"Because he tried to kill himself and he was saved. That's a big turning point in someone's life."

Nobody said anything. Ali felt herself becoming irritated. The word *saved* annoyed her. Stephen had a way of saying things that drew the subject back towards himself. He seemed to be talking about Daniel and being sympathetic towards him while gently pointing out his own role as saviour.

"Are we going to talk about this stuff for ever?" she suddenly said.

The others stared at her. Stephen's face had a mildly hurt expression.

"It's all we talk about. Daniel this, Daniel that. Haven't we got any other stuff going on?"

"Course we have," Stephen said. "I was just saying that I don't get why you two are so against helping the lad; holding out a friendly hand."

"Perhaps you should be his friend, if you're so keen," Jackson said.

"I wouldn't mind. Maybe we should invite him to come out with us."

"That's not a bad idea," Hannah said.

"What, *out* with us four?" Ali said.

"Yes. We could go for a drive or a drink or just anything. Just to give the lad a bit of a good time, a laugh."

"But that's stupid. There's me and you and Jackson and Hannah. He'd be the odd one out."

"It's not as if we're all hearts and roses every minute. Most of the time we sit talking. Why would it be so bad to have an extra person here?"

"I just don't think he's our responsibility," Jackson said, pulling at the leather band on his arm.

They continued talking, but Ali was thinking about what Stephen had said moments earlier. *It's not as if we're hearts and roses every minute.* It shouldn't surprise her that he could say such a thing. It was true. The foursome had been in trouble that night at Blackwood. Then they'd saved Daniel Feeny and that act seemed to cement them back together. They'd been carried along by it, that moment of intense excitement when something *real* had happened. They'd grabbed it hungrily, the attention, the kudos, the feeling that they were special because of what they'd done. But now, only weeks later, they'd eaten their fill and they were listless again, irritated with each other. There were no hearts and roses. The previous night they'd gone out for a drive to Harlow and stopped at a drive-through McDonald's. After they'd eaten, they parked up, and Ali heard frequent grumblings from the back of the car. She and Stephen weren't much better. They had a kiss and cuddle, but it was half-hearted, Stephen stopping to answer a text from Jonesy.

There were no hearts and flowers for them.

"Hey Ali, you're miles away!" Stephen said, touching her on the arm.

"Yeah, sorry," she said.

"Jonesy and I will take Daniel out next weekend. Might go to Brighton for the afternoon. There's a car rally there."

"I'm definitely going to pop in and see him after school," said Hannah.

56

"I'll come as well," mumbled Ali.

"Leave me out of it," Jackson said.

"We saved his life," Stephen said. "Shouldn't we try and do something about the *quality* of his life?"

Ali caught Jackson's eye. She held his glance for a moment. Stephen was beginning to sound like a priest. Then she had a feeling, more than a feeling, that Jackson was thinking the *same thing*. A tickle on her neck distracted her. She put her hand up and felt an itchy lump. The midges had got her.

She'd been bitten.

NINE

Two days later Ali and Hannah picked up handouts from different subject teachers and headed for Daniel Feeny's house. Hannah was walking in a sprightly way. Ali was lagging behind.

"Where's Jackson?" she said.

"Badminton."

"Oh."

They walked along. Ali was agitated. She had been building up to asking Hannah about how things were with Jackson. She wished she could come straight out with the question: *Do you think that you and Jackson will split up?* She had been rehearsing the words inside her head but she couldn't seem to say them out loud. She found herself saying something quite different.

"Are you going to be working in your mum's shop this summer?"

"Yeah, when the exams are finally over. How about you?"

Ali shrugged: "Not sure. Mum's got this friend who's opening a charity shop near the station? She needs some help to get it ready and Mum thinks it would be a good thing to do. No money, though."

"Charity shop might not be so bad. You could pick up lots of vintage stuff."

"And it'll look good on my CV. You know, for Cambridge."

"Do you think you'll actually go to university?"

Ali nodded.

"I wouldn't want to move away from Mum."

A car shot past, see-sawing over the speed hump. There was loud music coming from inside it. Ali thought she recognized the car. Some lads from school who drove round the streets at high speed pretending to be so grown up. She huffed. And then she thought about all of them driving here and there in Stephen's car. Did they think they were being grown up? What was the point of driving one way up a dual carriage simply to turn round and come back down the other side?

They walked in silence.

If only she could just *ask* Hannah. She and Jackson weren't exactly getting on very well. Hannah seemed especially dismissive of him now that he had said he definitely wasn't having anything to do with Daniel. That very lunch time she had virtually ignored him even though he was sitting three seats away. *What's up with her?* he'd mouthed to Ali and she had just shaken her head.

Hannah was humming something and seemed completely happy. She was going to ask her. She was going to be straight about it. She started to speak.

"Do you think that you and Jackson. . ."

But Hannah's ringtone sounded, so she stopped. Hannah answered the call and started to talk animatedly. It sounded as though the caller was her mum. As Hannah talked on, Ali let herself think about Jackson.

She had always liked him a lot. When the four of them went out in the car, she found herself agreeing with him, laughing at his jokes, having similar opinions about stuff. If she was honest, it was one of the reasons she liked going out in a foursome. He was there and she enjoyed being in his company, even if he had his girlfriend there with her big stripy bag and her moody ways. Meanwhile her own boyfriend sat as rigid as a broomstick in the driving seat, his conversation beginning and ending with cars and his old teacher Jonesy.

Then there was the touching.

In the last couple of weeks, since that night at Blackwood, Jackson was always touching Ali. It was never visible and never obvious and maybe, just maybe, it could have been accidental. Ali didn't think so. Sitting next to him and Hannah in the canteen, after an exam, she would feel one of his legs lean against hers. Then as he and Hannah stood up to go, his hand would touch her arm, sending a tingle along her skin. One day the previous week he had leaned across her to get the salt, and she felt the back of his arm touching the tips of her breasts.

It had given her the strangest feelings.

The night before last, with Stephen in the driver's seat and Hannah already in the back of the car, she and Jackson were both standing on the pavement looking at a poster for a movie on the side of a bus. It was something she wanted to see, and Jackson said he'd like to see it as well. Stephen tooted the horn impatiently, and as she opened the car door, she felt Jackson's hand on her arm, his fingers tightening for just a second. Then he got into the back seat. All the way home she had sat very still, her skin warm, the print of his hand still there on her arm.

Hannah's phone call had ended.

"Sorry, Ali, what were you saying? Weren't you going to ask me something?"

"It's not important," Ali said.

Daniel Feeny opened his front door. He had a white polystyrene brace round his neck. Ali was taken aback. Mrs Caine had described Daniel's injuries, but she hadn't expected them to be so obvious, so visible. His head was tilted back slightly. His long hair was in strings resting on the neck brace. He was pale. He looked nonplussed to see them.

"Hi, Daniel," Hannah said, her voice weighted with sympathy. "How are you? We've been worried about you."

He looked at Ali and she felt she had to say something.

"Mrs Caine asked us to pop round. . ."

"But we wanted to come anyway," Hannah said, "just to see if you were OK."

"I'm all right," he said, his voice uncertain.

"Any chance of coming in? Only I feel a bit of a div out here in the street," Hannah said.

"Yeah, sure," he said, stepping back, holding the door wide open.

Ali followed Hannah into Daniel's house.

"Dad's at work," he said. "Come into the kitchen. You want a coffee or something?"

They sat at a long table. Daniel spent a moment piling up some magazines that were there and Hannah took some papers out of her bag and laid them down. Ali looked round. The room was full of wooden cupboards that looked as though they'd just been polished. The work surfaces were clear. There were none of the usual things sitting about. No mug tree, bread bin or cutting boards. There wasn't even a spice rack.

Ali's eye was drawn to the fridge door, where there was an invitation to a wedding held on by a magnet. It was covered in silver balloons and had the words in raised gold lettering: *The Rainham Hotel, Saturday 19th June 4.30.*

"It's tidy in here," Hannah said, as Daniel filled a sleek silver kettle. "Don't tell us, you've got a servant."

"Dad's girlfriend, Debbie. She never stops cleaning. I'm frightened of sitting somewhere too long in case she tidies me away."

"Does she live with you?"

"Yes. What is this, an interrogation?"

"No, just interested."

Daniel went as if to nod but then stopped. A look of pain flickered across his face. His hand went up to the brace and fiddled with it.

"That looks uncomfortable," Hannah said.

"It is."

"You could do with a haircut. You know what? I could cut it for you. When you get the brace off. I'm really good at cutting hair."

Daniel gave a polite smile and went back to organizing the cups, spooning coffee into each one.

"Stephen and his friend Jones came round on Sunday," he said.

"*Jonesy,*" Ali said. "Actually it's his old teacher from school."

"Well, it was good of them. I didn't expect people to bother. . ."

"Why not? Just because some scumbags in school..." Hannah said.

"Anyway, Stephen's all right. He's your boyfriend, Ali? Right?"

Ali nodded.

"He's a good bloke."

Daniel handed them the hot drinks. He sat down at the table and there was an uneasy silence.

"About that night up at Blackwood..." Hannah said.

Ali made a face at Hannah.

"You're blunt," Daniel said.

"He doesn't want to talk about stuff like that," Ali said.

"He might. It's not like we don't *know* about it."

Daniel was quiet for a minute. Ali felt awkward. She wished she wasn't there. Looking after Daniel when he was in trouble was all right. Actually *being* with him was something else. She pulled one of the magazines on the table towards her. It was a car magazine. Stephen had a pile of them in his room.

"Stephen gets this."

"I know," Daniel said.

"He likes cars."

"Understatement," Hannah said.

"All right, he loves cars. He lives and breathes for cars."

"I'm getting a jeep when I'm seventeen. Dad's getting me one. Stephen said he might know somewhere we can get one."

"Anyway, about that night. At Blackwood. Do you not want to talk about it?" Hannah said, leaning her chin on her knuckles.

Daniel laughed and then moved his head carefully to the side, putting a finger between the brace and his neck. Ali noticed the redness then. The skin looked as though it had been sunburned. She looked away.

"I don't mind talking about it. Most people don't ask me. They keep quiet. They don't know what to say. *Why'd you try and top yourself?* It's not an easy question to ask."

"Why'd you try and top yourself?" Hannah said.

Ali gasped, but Daniel just smiled. He looked at the pile of school handouts lying on the table. He flicked across them with his finger.

"I'm not completely sure. It seemed like a good idea at the time?"

"Now you're just joking," Hannah said.

"Because I felt like crap. Like I was in this dark box. Like I had no air to breathe. I couldn't see a way out. Am I being too metaphorical?"

"Meta what? What's that when it's at home?" Hannah said, adopting a dumb expression.

"I felt like I just wanted to escape."

"Because of stuff at school?"

"Maybe."

Hannah seemed rapt. She was staring at him.

Ali coughed. "Stephen says you're going to Brighton on Saturday for a car rally."

"Was Stephen the guy who actually *cut* the rope?" Daniel said.

Ali nodded but looked away with embarrassment. The mention of the *rope* was too blunt. It made a picture in her head of Daniel hanging, his feet dangling in mid-air.

"Just as well he could climb. Just as well you were all there."

"Why don't you come back to school?" Hannah said. "To hell with all the others. You could hang around with me and Ali."

"And Jackson," Ali said.

Daniel shook his head. "I'm finished with that place. I've been pushed around too much there. I don't want to go back and have them pity me."

"You shouldn't let them push you around. Just stand your ground. Come back to school. We can help you!"

He shook his head. "It's too late now. If I go somewhere new, I can start again. I can stand up for myself. At least that's what my dad and Debbie say."

"What? Be a hard man?" Hannah said.

"Maybe." Daniel was smiling now. "Maybe I'll be like Stephen."

"Stephen's not a hard man!" Ali said.

"How did he get his scar?"

"An angry kid and a kitchen knife," Ali said.

"Anyway, it'll be better if I go somewhere new."

"Well, you're definitely too young to get married!" Hannah said, pointing at the invitation on the fridge door.

"Right. Funny. That's my dad's. He and Debbie are getting married."

"Oh."

They talked on, and after a while, Ali started to make faces at Hannah. Hadn't they stayed long enough?

"You will come again?" Daniel said, as he walked them to the front door.

"Course we will," Hannah said.

"If there's time..." Ali said.

"Surely you've got time for someone who tried to top himself?"

Daniel was tugging at his neck brace, trying to move it. For a second Ali was reminded of the moment when they dropped him on to the grass at Blackwood and someone shone a torch on his neck. The sight of the rope clinging to Daniel's throat had shocked them all. He had been seconds from death. Now he just looked puffed and uncomfortable, the neck brace like a heavy reminder of what he'd tried to do.

"I've got the time," Hannah said, smiling.

"Um. . ." Ali echoed.

When they were almost at Hannah's street, Ali managed to ask the question.

"You and Jackson. How's that going?"

"What do you mean?"

"Are you getting on all right?"

Hannah shrugged.

"Only I wondered if maybe – if you were on the brink of breaking up? You always seem so fed up."

There, she'd said it. She held her breath waiting for an answer.

"Oh, you know. Things are OK. You know what it's like being in a relationship. You and Stephen aren't exactly Romeo and Juliet these days."

"Well, no."

Hannah's comment floored her. She and Stephen had never been Romeo and Juliet.

"We get along. For the moment."

"So you don't think it's serious?" Ali said.

"God, Ali. I'm seventeen. I'm not looking to get engaged. I like him. We have fun *most of the time*."

"I was only asking."

Ali watched Hannah go off down her turning. She walked on to her own street, feeling disgruntled. Why was it not possible to have a straightforward conversation with Hannah? Why could she not just say, *I like Jackson. If he's not important to you, give him up and let me have him.*

Why couldn't she just say that?

The next day after school, she waited round for Hannah in the atrium. After standing for a few seconds gazing at a display of art on the wall, she felt a cool hand on the back of her neck. It sent a ripple across her skin. She didn't turn round because she knew it was Jackson. After a couple of seconds, he stepped forward. He had his badminton racquet in his hand. "*See you*," he said in a half-whisper and walked off. She looked around, foolishly, feeling as though she'd just done something indecent in a public place. Using the palm of her hand, she smoothed the skin on the back of her neck.

When Hannah hadn't appeared ten minutes later, she wandered back towards the classroom where her last lesson had been. Mrs Caine was tidying up books and handouts.

"Is Hannah around?" she said.

"Hi, Alison. No, Hannah popped off ten minutes before the bell. I had a few things for Daniel and she said she didn't mind taking them to him."

Ali walked away from the classroom.

Hannah had gone to Daniel's *on her own*?

TEN

The trip to Brighton had been a success.

Stephen was pleased with himself. He talked about it for ages that evening. Ali listened with patience. It had been Daniel's first time out without the brace on his neck. He had been good company, Stephen said. He wasn't such a bad lad. He was quiet, but he chatted a little. And he knew a fair bit about some of the cars they saw.

Ali was in Stephen's room with him, lying on his bed. His bedside clock showed the time: 21.09. It was still light outside, but Stephen had closed his venetian blinds so the room was in shadows.

"He kept offering to pay," Stephen said. "Petrol, food, drinks. I told him to put his wallet away."

"His dad's well off," Ali said.

"When we took him back home, his dad came out and started thanking us. He's getting married in a couple of weeks. His girlfriend was there. His dad was really loud, talking and joking. Jonesy said that maybe that's why Daniel is so quiet. He can't get a word in edgeways."

"Um. . ."

All this talking about Daniel was getting in the way of Ali's new drive to be passionate with Stephen. She was intent on making her relationship with him more exciting, more interesting, more worth the bother. If only he'd stop going on about Daniel.

Her clothes were undone. She was on her side with her knee across his legs. He was lying on his back, completely relaxed, his hands behind his head. They'd messed around for a while, kissing and touching, but it was Stephen who had drawn back, pulled away from her. He pointed down to the floor, indicating his mum and dad's presence in the room below.

"I think Daniel needs someone to give him a boost. When we were on our way back, we stopped in traffic on the high street and there was a group of young lads hanging round outside McDonald's. Daniel kind of shrank back, turned his head away from them. He said they were from school. He seemed to visibly curl up. Jonesy said afterwards that maybe he needs some physical training. Boxing or weight training?"

"You're going to try and make him into a tough guy? Won't that just get him into fights? I thought you were against fighting."

"No, you don't get it. The boxing or weights doesn't make you a *fighter*. They just give you the confidence you need to face off these kids who think they can wind you up. I should know. I did a fair bit of bullying in my time. If a kid stands up to you, just physically stands his ground, looks you in the eye, squares his shoulders – that's enough."

"You're going to change him?" Ali said, rolling away from Stephen, doing her shirt up, straightening her skirt.

"Why not? We all need someone to help us. When I was younger, when I got this –" Stephen pointed to the scar on his face – "it was Jonesy who helped me. He was my English teacher then. *Mr Jones*. He was only young but completely bald. Like his hair had fallen out overnight. His mobile kept going off in the middle of lessons and he'd blame one of us, but he couldn't keep a straight face. He had this old car. A Ford. He called it vintage. It was always breaking down, and he used to pay kids fifty pence to push so that it would jump-start. One day he said to me, *Unless you keep your temper under control, you'll end up with a face like a noughts and crosses game*."

Ali lay back. She folded her arms. She'd heard bits of this before.

"He lived a few streets away from me and let me work on his car at weekends. It gave me some breathing space, and I suppose the others, the hard boys, they mostly moved on."

Outside, in the street, a car hooted gently.

"Then when I was about seventeen I got in trouble again. Some of the old mob turned up. I got drawn back in. I ended up hanging round with them again. One day, out of the blue, Jonesy turned up at my house. He told me I was a loser and that I'd end up in prison or worse. He told me to empty my pockets out on to the table. If anyone else had said it, I would have told them to get lost, but because he was my old teacher, I just sort of did what he said. I pulled the usual stuff out of one pocket; then I realized that I had this flick knife in the other."

Ali pictured Jonesy with his shiny bald head standing in Stephen's kitchen, like a head of year searching through someone's bag for cigarettes or dope.

"I held the knife in my hand and I said, *I'd never use this. Not after what that kid did to me. It's just for protection.* He took it from me and pressed the button so that the blade shot out.

Then he upended it and offered it back to me. *Here,* he said, *I want you to hold this against my chest. I want you to know what it feels like to have someone's life in your hands. Go on! Go on!* he said. He made me hold the knife and then he pulled my hand towards him so that the blade was in between the buttons of his shirt."

Stephen stopped for a minute, as though he was remembering the scene.

"Did you put the knife down?"

Stephen shook his head. "Jonesy held it there. He says, *Now you could kill me if you wanted. How does that feel?*"

"How did it feel?"

"I felt sick. I actually *felt* sick, and he let go of my hand, and then he left the house."

"Is that when you started hanging round with him?"

"No, that was months later. He called me up and took me stock car racing. He never mentioned the knife."

"And you've been on the straight and narrow ever since!" Ali said, trying to lighten the atmosphere, feeling *awkward* at Stephen's honesty.

"Sort of."

She lay there in the twilight of the room. Stephen felt hot beside her. She put her arm across his chest. His ribs felt hard and sharp. The atmosphere seemed to have changed. He was tense. He sat up, making her arm slide off him.

"I know you don't like Daniel, but I feel responsible for him. When you stop someone from killing themselves, you kind of owe it to them to see that their life is a bit better. Don't you?"

Ali sighed. He was obsessed with this whole thing. How was

71

she supposed to have an interesting relationship with him if he only ever thought about one thing?

"I have to go," she said, sitting up. "I told Mum I'd watch a DVD with her."

"All this talking about me. What about you? Glad the exams are finished?"

She nodded.

"How do you think you've done? Good enough for Cambridge?"

"I don't know! I don't even know if I want to go to *Cambridge*."

"Don't bite my head off!"

"Sorry."

"When are you starting at the charity shop?"

"A week on Monday. But I won't be working there every day. School's not quite over yet. I've got to go back in for a few things. Oh, and there's the leavers' assembly. . ."

She noticed a card lying flat under Stephen's mobile on his bedside table. There were silver balloons at each corner. She picked it up. *The Rainham Hotel, Saturday 19th June 4.30.*

"How come you got this?"

"Oh. Daniel's dad insisted that I took it when I dropped him off. He says we should all go. The four of us. I took it, but I didn't think anyone would *want* to go."

"God, no!" Ali said.

"It was nice of him to ask, though."

"Um."

"What DVD are you watching?"

"Not sure. It's Mum's choice."

"I can't see you tomorrow because I said I'd take Daniel over to Jonesy's. I thought he might be able to talk about the suicide stuff with him. He's not from your school, so he's kind of objective?"

She went down the stairs.

"See you in the evening?" he said.

"Maybe," she said.

She walked into her house and found it silent. No sound of her mum or dad. No television on or music from upstairs. She clicked on the hall light. On the table was a note.

Something's up with Gran's sink, so Dad and I are going over to fix it. Will call you later. Mum

Ali sighed. It was almost ten o'clock on Saturday night. Her exams were over. She had a boyfriend and other friends, and yet she was on her own with nothing to do and nowhere to go.

ELEVEN

There was no reason to go into school, but Ali went anyway. By Wednesday she was fed up being at home, so she took in some books and handouts and returned them to a couple of teachers. The younger years were milling around, looking hot and bothered, carrying bags that looked as though they were full of bricks instead of books. She walked in and out of her old form room and looked around at the messy displays and the piles of papers and exercise books on the teacher's desk.

She went and visited the careers block even though she knew that she was going to the sixth-form college in the autumn. She flicked through the folders: nursing, teaching, catering, social work, police force, engineering. It was all years away. It was like looking into the distance and seeing a road go on for ever. In the middle of that road was Cambridge. She tried to picture what Cambridge would be like. It was a pretty old town, she knew that. Lots of tourists went there. She knew it was prestigious. Mrs Caine had told her that it would be like a doorway opening on to a whole new world of possibilities. She'd asked Mrs Caine where she'd gone to university and the teacher's mouth had twisted and she'd said, "East Anglia, sadly." Ali had no idea what the difference was.

Hannah was clear about her future. She would work in her

mum's hairdresser's. "Not just as a hairdresser," she'd said, "as a business partner." Stephen was in the building society, but only until he had enough money to start up his own small business buying and selling cars. "Rare cars, not just any old rubbish," he'd said. And Jackson was going to university at Brighton. Definitely. He was going to study history.

What was she going to do with her life beyond university? She thought about this as she drifted through the quiet corridors, listening to the snatches of lessons going on in the classrooms. Did she have any idea what her future was going to be like? Her dad worked down at Purfleet docks, but he wasn't a docker. He designed computer programs that enabled the docks to function. Her mum was the practice manager in a local doctor's surgery. What would she be? She had no idea.

Over the next few weeks she would be working in St Mark's Hospice Charity Shop. It was due to open in a month and she was helping to set it up. Cleaning and painting the shop; sorting through old clothes and things that people had donated. She'd be working alongside women who were positively ancient. The idea didn't fill her with great enthusiasm.

She found herself heading for the exit. It was coming up to lunch time but she didn't feel hungry. She wondered where Hannah was. Most probably in her mum's shop washing hair or sweeping up or sitting at the till and answering the phone. Hannah had said that she could go and join her there. *Have a coffee! Have a haircut!* But she didn't feel like either of these.

She headed for home. When she got to her street, she felt restless and agitated. She kept on walking. She went past her front door to the other end of the street. She turned a corner, then another. Five minutes later she found herself at the top of Jackson's street.

She walked along until she was outside his door. She hesitated. She knew that Hannah was at work. What reason did she have to see Jackson? She pictured herself explaining it later to Stephen or Hannah. *I was just passing... I was at a loose end...* The one true thing was the thing she couldn't say. *I was desperate to see him.* And then it came to her. Why not just tell him how she felt?

She rang the bell before she could change her mind and he opened the door in seconds, as though he'd been standing on the other side waiting for her.

"Hi, Ali," he said. "Come in."

"I was just at school," she said, as if in explanation.

"The uniform gave it away," he said.

She was still wearing the blue skirt, the white blouse, the striped tie, the flat shoes. He, on the other hand, was wearing faded khaki shorts and a sleeveless T-shirt. On his feet he had flip-flops. Beside her, he looked underdressed.

"Yeah, I just went in to take some stuff back..."

"You look hot. Have a drink."

Jackson walked down his hallway and she followed. There was music coming from the kitchen and someone was singing along with it. It wasn't the first time she had been in his house. A couple of times, after they'd been for a drive, he'd invited them all in. They'd ordered some pizzas and taken them up to Jackson's loft room.

"Hello, Alison," Mrs Jackson said, loudly.

Jackson's mum was washing dishes, wearing a plastic apron

covered in cats. On her hands she had scarlet rubber gloves.

"Hi."

Mrs Jackson was doing a half-dance with the music, placing washed plates into a dish stacker and then singing out loud. Jackson rolled his eyes and Ali smiled. It all seemed so normal. As though she was meant to be there.

"Coke? Water? Orange juice?" Jackson said, rattling through the bottles in the door of the fridge.

"Some orange juice would be good," she said, using a hand to lean on the back of a kitchen chair.

Jackson poured the drinks and then handed one to Ali. The song stopped and there was a moment's silence before another one started.

"This is a madhouse. Let's get out of here," Jackson said and walked out of the kitchen. He obviously expected her to follow, so she gave Mrs Jackson a shaky smile and went after him.

Jackson's room was untidy. His bed was unmade and had clothes draped across it. Above his bed, on the slanted roof of the loft, was a giant window that was partly open. A breeze wafted through it, ruffling a set of windchimes that Ali hadn't noticed before. She went towards an old settee that was in the opposite corner. It was where they'd all sat eating pizza. Jackson pulled the chair from his desk and placed it opposite her. He sat down.

"What you been doing?"

"This and that," she said.

"Hannah's at work."

"I know."

"Stephen all right?"

"Oh, you know."

"How did Brighton go?"

"They had a good time. You know Jonesy went."

"A whole day with Daniel Feeny."

She finished her drink and placed her glass on the floor. Jackson's legs were directly in front of her and for a moment she couldn't take her eyes off them. The skin was tanned and covered in fine hairs. She had an urge to feel them, to run her fingers along them. When she looked up at Jackson, he was staring at her. The chimes tinkled from across the room. She looked away, acutely aware of how close he was. Maybe this was the time to tell him. Right at that moment. Just blurt the words out. *I like you. I've liked you for a long time. I want you to break up with Hannah and be with me.*

"What are you going to do all summer? Are you going to get a job?" he said.

"No. Mum knows this woman who's opening a new charity shop. I'm going to help her. It'll be an experience. You know, good for the CV and Cambridge and stuff."

He nodded.

"What about you?" she said.

"I'll be working on my brother's house in Brighton. I'm going on Saturday for a few days to help him knock down the old conservatory."

"And you're going to live with him if you get into uni down there?"

"If? Course I'll get in. I got it all planned out."

"What about Hannah?"

He smiled and gave a shrug. "It's a long time off. Who knows what can happen."

Tell him now. Say the words. *I like you. I've liked you for a long time.*

"Thing is," she said, pulling the conversation back, "I wanted to talk to you about something."

He was leaning forward, his elbows on his thighs. His eyes seemed to be boring into her. She could say it, just say the words. She *had* to say it. A breeze blew into the room, making the windchimes scatter and then chink and ping as they settled back together. Something worried her, though. What if she said what she felt and Jackson was shocked or embarrassed? What if he were to laugh or recoil from her? Then she would know that all the looks and the touching added up to nothing.

"What?" he said. "Is something up with Stephen?"

She relaxed. This was better. This was a safer way of talking about her feelings.

"Yes," she said. "That was what I was going to say. I'm thinking of breaking up with him and I wondered what you thought."

"Um..."

"He and I aren't really right for each other. We never were."

"How long you been thinking about this?"

"A while. Since before that night ... up at Blackwood. When..."

"The night Daniel..."

"Ever since then it's been hard. There hasn't been the right time. It's like everyone sees us as this *couple*. And I've been carried along by it," she said, the words coming out freely, "and Stephen's been different since then? He seems *driven* by this thing with Daniel. He took him to Brighton on Saturday. He took

79

him to see Jonesy on Sunday. And he saw him last night, took him to some boxing club."

"He does seem to be on a sort of crusade."

"So, I've hardly seen him. But you know what? I don't really mind. It's as though I'm glad he's got stuff to do."

"So it's not about Daniel. You're fed up with him."

She nodded. "What about you and Hannah?" she said, nervously.

"You know. Me and Hannah are very up and down."

Her mouth felt dry. From downstairs she could hear the faint sound of music. Jackson put his glass down on the floor.

"But do you think you'll last?"

"What's happening with me and Hannah is not important. If you and Stephen aren't getting on, then you need to do something about it."

"Stephen's a good bloke, but he's not for me."

"You have to talk to him," Jackson said, his voice in a half whisper.

He was leaning towards her. She couldn't make eye contact, so she looked at his wrist, at the leather band that was on it. She reached out and touched it.

"I always liked this," she said, her voice husky.

She glanced up at his face. They were so close that his eyes looked black. She raised her other hand. More than anything she wanted to touch his cheek.

"You should tell Stephen what you're feeling. Be honest with him."

She let her hand drop and sat back. "I don't know what to say."

"Just tell him what you said to me. Say you don't think you're right for each other."

"Is that what you would do? If it was you and Hannah?" she said, raising her eyes to his, looking searchingly at him.

"This is about you and Stephen."

Jackson reached across and put his hand on hers. He squeezed it gently. The touch felt hot like fire on her skin. She swallowed, looking at her empty glass on the floor, wishing she had some drink left.

"I should go."

She stood up. She picked up her glass and walked ahead of him down the stairs.

"Don't worry about Stephen. Talk to him. Make a decision. You'll sort it out," Jackson said.

Minutes later she was out in the street heading for home.

You'll sort it out, he'd said.

Would she?

She spent the next couple of days alone. On Thursday she had been due to see Stephen, but she sent him a text to say that she wasn't feeling well. Hannah called her. They chatted, but Hannah didn't say that Jackson had mentioned her visit. Ridiculously, stupidly, she thought it meant something. The fact that he hadn't told his girlfriend about their talk made her feel hopeful.

On Friday morning she lay in bed long after her mum and dad had gone to work. When she got up and went downstairs, she saw a small padded envelope on the hall table. She picked it up and saw her name and address in neat handwriting. She was puzzled. She'd not bought anything online or sent for anything.

She held it for a moment and felt the contents. Then she opened it. Inside was a sheet of paper and a slim tissue packet the length of a watch strap. She read the words.

Ali, I know you liked this. J

She pulled at the tissue paper, using her nails to pick at the sticky tape. When it came off, she held a new leather band in her hand. It was identical to Jackson's. She draped it across her wrist. He had *bought* it for her. He had gone out and bought it especially for her.

She sat on the bottom stair and smiled delightedly.

The leather bands were a matching pair. She closed her eyes with pleasure.

TWELVE

The charity shop was coated in dust. Ali had a mask over her nose and she was up a small stepladder. In her hand she had a wet duster and it was her job to wipe the shelves clean. Her back was aching and she had the beginning of a headache. The woman in charge, Mrs Lumsden, was in the back room making a cup of tea. Ali could hear cups clinking. She pulled her mobile out of her pocket to look at the time. It was twenty-five past two.

At that moment the shop door opened and the traffic sounds got louder. She looked round. Two women came in. One was wearing a tracksuit and had white curly hair. The other was younger, her hair in a ponytail. Behind them, on the road, a giant lorry was wheezing, waiting in a queue of traffic.

"Hello, girls!" Mrs Lumsden called from the back room.

The women answered and Ali gave them a wave and went back to the shelves. She reached across to the far corner. Her shirtsleeve rode up and she saw the leather band on her wrist. It made her feel good. A second later she sighed.

She didn't know what to do.

She would break up with Stephen. She was certain of that.

Why hadn't she done it already? Why not do it today? She was supposed to be meeting Stephen from work just after five-thirty. He wanted to go for a drink with her. He'd been spending a lot of time with Jonesy and Daniel and he wanted to make it up to her. The building society where he worked was a five-minute walk away.

Why wait any longer to finish it?

It was five days since she'd been in Jackson's room. That was when she had really decided. When the gift of the leather band arrived a couple of days later, she had felt completely convinced that it was the right thing to do. There was something between her and Jackson. She felt it every time she was near to him, some kind of heat, some kind of invisible pull that drew her to him. The only way anything was going to happen was if the foursome broke apart.

The previous night she'd woken up at three o'clock feeling restless, unable to sleep. She'd stretched out and thought about Jackson's naked legs and pictured him lying alongside her. It gave her an ache in the pit of her stomach. It was hot in her bedroom and she'd thrown off the sheet and her nightie. She'd closed her eyes and lain on her front, her face into the pillow. She'd imagined Jackson's fingers on her back, his breath on her ear. Eventually, after turning this way and that, she slipped back into a light sleep. When she woke up that morning, she resolved to go and see Stephen straightaway, before he went to work, before she set off for her first day in the charity shop. She intended to go up to his front door and ask him to come outside while she told him. *I think we should break up*, she was going to say. But when it came to doing it, she felt a flutter of anxiety.

What if she was wrong and Jackson felt nothing for her? What if he just saw her as a friend? If she gave Stephen up and he didn't break up with Hannah, she would know that she had misread the situation. Hannah and Jackson would go back to going out by themselves, and apart from the school leavers' assembly, Ali would have no reason to see him all summer.

She came backwards down the stepladder. She'd finished the shelves. She pulled the mask off her face and let it hang round her neck.

"Here you are, dear," Mrs Lumsden said, holding a mug of steaming tea. "Margaret, this is Alison, who's helping us to get the shop ready. Alison, that's Margaret with the curly hair and that's Sheila."

"Hi," Ali said, sitting down and blowing across the top of the tea.

"Are you Shirley Rose's granddaughter?" Sheila said.

Ali nodded.

"I thought so. I saw you with your mum in Marks and Spencer's. How is she?"

"She's good."

"What about your gran?"

"She's good. A bit forgetful, but. . ."

"I heard she had dementia. I was so sorry to hear it. Shirley was such a live wire!"

"She's coping quite well."

"That's good," Mrs Lumsden said. "There's a lot they can do for dementia nowadays. Tablets and the like."

"I'm on new tablets for my blood pressure," the other woman, Margaret, said.

They carried on talking, and Ali smiled and nodded while drinking her tea. The leather band slipped up and down her arm as she drank. She'd been wrong about it being the exact same as Jackson's. It wasn't. It fastened differently. Jackson's was tied in an elaborate knot. He wore it all the time. Hers had a button and a loop that went over it. So it was easy and quick to put on and take off.

If only she could be decisive.

There was another thing that was holding her back, though. Stephen lived along her road and she would have to face him from time to time. She didn't know if he would be upset or not, but it would be embarrassing to come out of her house and see him working on his car. And what if, in the end, she came out of her house with Jackson? What would Stephen feel like then?

Alison stood up. Mrs Lumsden stopped talking and looked up at her.

"I've done the shelves. Shall I make a start on the windows?"

"Yes, dear. There's a spray in the back. Give them a good clean."

She worked on the shop windows. It was an awkward job because she had to edge between the previous shop display material and the window. The shop had been used by different charities on and off for years. Now it was having a makeover and would be reopened in a couple of weeks.

She stopped for a minute. The main difficulty in cleaning the windows was getting off odd little patches of glitter, like the stuff that people spray on at Christmastime to give a festive feeling. It must have been on there for six months. She pushed two fingers into the duster and rubbed small circles on the window.

That was when she noticed Hannah, across the road, in the bus shelter. A bus had just moved off and the shelter was almost empty. Daniel Feeny was there. It took her a moment to be sure, because he looked different. His long hair was gone. He'd had a short spiky cut. The two of them were sitting on one of the little half seats in the shelter and he was leaning down and speaking into Hannah's ear. Ali stopped what she was doing and stared at them.

She noticed that his neck brace was gone. Stephen had told her that he had stopped wearing it the day he took him to Brighton. Daniel looked different, really different. He was wearing cut-offs and a loose shirt. Apart from that one time in his kitchen, Ali had only ever seen him in school uniform. Except for that night up at Blackwood. What had he been wearing then? She had no idea, no memory of the clothes. It was just over four weeks since he'd tried to kill himself and all she could remember was the twist of rope that seemed embedded in his neck.

Now here he was looking confident and relaxed.

Hannah laughed at something he said and he leaned forward with his elbows on his knees. Hannah nudged him but he ignored her. Hannah nudged him again really hard and he wobbled as though he might fall off the seat.

He didn't, though. He turned to Hannah and kissed her on the mouth.

"You all right, dear?"

She heard Mrs Lumsden's voice.

"Yeah, I'm fine," she said.

"Only you could pack up now. You've done loads this afternoon. We're really grateful. We'll see you later in the week."

"Right," Ali said, her eyes staring out of the window as Hannah and Daniel embraced. "I'll get off."

Hannah gave Daniel a little push and then a bus pulled up and blocked Ali's view. She edged out of the window and walked into the back of the shop, where Sheila and Margaret were upending black plastic bags of clothes. She picked her bag up.

"See you," she said.

"How about Wednesday?" Mrs Lumsden said. "We'll probably do a bit of painting then."

"OK," Ali said, holding the door open, keen to get out of the shop.

The bus began to move away. Ali stood still on the pavement opposite. She looked along the windows to see if they had got on the bus. She couldn't make them out. Finally the bus moved into the traffic and there were Hannah and Daniel, still sitting on the seats in the shelter.

Hannah looked up and saw her.

Ali checked on the traffic and then crossed the road towards them. Daniel looked awkward. His hand went up to his neck as though the brace was still there. Hannah stood up, looking brisk, businesslike. Looking as if she was ready for an argument.

"Hi," Ali said.

"All right?" Hannah said.

"Hi, Ali," Daniel said.

Were they going to pretend that nothing had happened?

"What's going on?"

Daniel looked down at the ground.

"Oh, come on, Ali. You knew me and Jackson weren't getting on well."

"How long's *this* been going on?"

"A few days. A week at most. I've hardly seen Jackson. He's gone to his brother's."

"Have you told him?" Ali said.

"When he gets back on Wednesday."

Ali turned her eyes on Daniel. She looked back at Hannah and made a face. "Are you just feeling sorry for him? Because of what happened?"

"I am here," Daniel said. "You can include me in the conversation."

"It's nothing to do with that. I never really knew him before. I like him. I like him a lot," Hannah said, one of her hands dropping to touch Daniel's hair.

"I don't get it."

How could Hannah choose Daniel over Jackson?

"What do you think of his new haircut? All my own work!"

Ali shrugged. Daniel was patting the top of his hair down. Behind her she could hear a bus pulling up. Daniel stood up and put his arm around Hannah's shoulder, straightening the collar of the shirt she was wearing.

"Our bus," he said.

Ali stared at him. Then her eyes dropped to his neck. The redness around it had faded, but there was still a raw, pink mark there.

"Don't fall out with me," Hannah said.

She took Ali's wrist in a gesture of warmth. She had her mouth open to say something else when her eye settled on the leather band that Ali was wearing. Hannah looked up. Her eyes seemed to fix on Ali's, and then she gave a little nod. Ali felt as though Hannah knew everything in that instant.

"Come on," Daniel called from the bus platform.

"Come into the shop for a haircut. Mum'll do it. Free of charge.

Maybe even some streaks," Hannah said, a knowing smile playing about her lips.

She stepped on to the bus. Ali watched the two of them heading for the stairs and disappearing from sight. Disconcerted, she pushed the leather band up her arm so that her shirt covered it. She started to walk. The clock on the station front showed 17.25. She was going to meet Stephen at half past. They were supposed to be having a drink, catching up with what was happening, he said. So what if she had a leather band like Jackson's? It wasn't up to Hannah to jump to conclusions. Much more important was the fact that Hannah was going to finish it with Jackson on Wednesday.

This was the moment. This was the time to end it with Stephen.

She could see the corner of the building society where he worked. She quickened her step. She couldn't let this moment go. She was fired up. It would be quick and simple. *I think we should break up. I want to be on my own. I'm sorry if it hurts your feelings, but I'm not ready for a serious relationship.*

The doors to the building society opened, and as if by magic, there he was, standing waiting for her. He was wearing a suit, and a breeze blew the jacket open to reveal his shirt and tie, and around his neck, the nametag that he had to wear every day at work. She'd looked at it often enough. Beside a solemn photo was his name: *Stephen J Grainger.*

He saw her coming and raised his arm to wave at her.

She was going to finish it. She put her head down and walked towards him.

THIRTEEN
Year Thirteen

The ghost came again. Twice in two days.

Alison had gone off to sleep easily but woke up soon after. There was a noise. She thought she might be dreaming but slowly realized that she wasn't. There was a sound of tapping, of scratching. It lasted a few seconds, then stopped. Then it started again. She lay very still for a long time. Her head was fuzzy and there were images appearing in her mind like a slideshow; fragments of leftover dreams. Still the sound was there; scratching like nails on metal. She turned over, opening her eyes. The bedside clock read 01.41. The room was thick with dark, but when she looked towards the window it was lighter, moonlight seeping in like a mist. Or maybe it was part of one of her dreams. She closed her eyes tightly, her duvet pulled across her head.

The scratching stopped.

She counted her own breaths. Her chest lifted and fell. Nine... Nineteen... Thirty-one... Forty-three... She listened hard for any noise, any sense of movement. Her mouth and jaw were tight. Was it gone? Was it over?

A cry sounded. A sob.

She instantly sat up. She scrambled backwards, up to the head of the bed. With a trembling hand she clawed out for the bedside lamp, knocking it over.

A noise from her parents' room made her look round.

She set the lamp upright and turned it on. She grabbed a book that was on her bedside table. She was still for a moment, the flat of her hand on her chest, trying to stem the panic.

A couple of knocks sounded on her room door. Then it opened.

"I thought I heard you," her mum said, yawning. "Can't sleep?"

She shook her head, turning a page in the book as if to make it convincing.

"Maybe you'll sleep better when your A-levels are over."

"Definitely," she said, her voice cracking with dryness.

"See you in the morning."

The door closed and she heard her mum's footsteps down the hallway.

Would she ever sleep well again? She thought not.

She left the light on and lay down again. Her mind went back to the previous evening, when Jackson had met them in the sports centre café at Blackwood.

Alison had got there early and Stephen and Jackson arrived moments later. They'd nodded stiffly at each other in the car park and she waited as they came in and walked across the seating area. Stephen was still in his work suit and took a moment to straighten his trousers before he sat down. Jackson sat opposite her. She allowed herself a good look at him while Stephen fussed with the menu. Jackson had lost some weight in the last couple of years. His face looked longer and sharper. His hair was untidy. She glanced at his wrist. There was no leather band, just a bulky black watch.

All of a sudden he looked up at her and held her glance. She felt her mouth go dry and she cleared her throat.

"I'll get some drinks," she said.

She got up and bought some cans. As she was paying for them, she looked round and saw that the two of them were sitting stonily side by side, not speaking. Stephen was looking pointedly at his watch.

"How've you both been?" she said, putting the drinks on the table.

"All right," Stephen said.

Jackson just shrugged. She noticed his skin then. It was red and angry where he'd been shaving. There were sore spots and a rash on his neck.

Stephen pulled the ring on his can and got straight to the point.

"We agreed not to talk about this again," he said.

Jackson nodded.

"So what's it all about? I've got somewhere to be."

"Let Jackson speak," Alison said, quietly.

"I've been working in this bar in Brighton," Jackson said. "I thought if I went somewhere else I could. . ."

"I thought you went to college down there."

"I had a place, but I couldn't face it."

"Spare me the life story," Stephen said.

Alison stared at Stephen. The scar on his cheek had faded even more in the last two years and was whiter than the rest of his skin. He looked bloodless.

"I'll make it quick," Jackson said. "I've come back because I'm going to go to the police. I thought you should know. I'm going to tell them everything. Obviously it will involve both of you. I'm sorry about that. I will try and take the whole blame. . ."

Stephen was silent. Alison felt her stomach crumple.

"Why?" she said.

"Because I can't live with it any more. I've tried. I just can't. It makes me feel sick most of the time. I've been sick one way or another ever since. I can't eat, I can't sleep. . ."

Stephen leaned forward. "Do you think it's been easy for me? It happened. No one meant for it to happen like that, but it did. What's the point of dragging it all up again? It's not going to bring him back, is it?"

Alison looked at a spot on the table. Jackson was across from her. She could feel his closeness. His knees were almost touching hers. Like the way it had been when she had seen him in his loft that summer two years before.

"You have to deal with it your way. I have to deal with it mine. I'm just telling you in case you need to get a solicitor or something."

"Why would we want a solicitor?" Ali said.

"I don't know what the police will do. They might arrest you."

"I'm not listening to this. This is rubbish. What sort of game are you playing? If you want to go to the law, why do you need to say anything about us?" Stephen said, his voice loud and angry.

Alison shushed him. She looked around. There were half a dozen other people in the café.

"Because you drove the car," Jackson hissed. "You brought Daniel to that yard. I couldn't have got him there on my own."

Stephen sat back with a sigh. The puff had gone out of him.

"This is priceless," he said. "The police will interview us all, but you know who'll take the blame? Me. I was the eldest, I was the one with the car. You two were at school. With my record, it'll look like I was the instigator. I'll go down."

"No, because I'll tell the truth. I have to tell the truth. . ."

Stephen stood up. He pushed the chair back so that it wobbled as if it might fall. Then he walked away. The door closed behind him. Alison watched him cross the car park. She looked at his new car. It was silver, but she had no idea what make. It looked flashier than the one he had driven two years before.

When she looked away, Jackson was staring back at her.

"I can't live with it any more," he said.

95

She put her hand out and covered one of his. She could feel his bones, the sharpness of his knuckles. He didn't seem like the same boy.

"How can you?" he said. "How can you go on every day knowing what we did? How can you not suffer?"

She couldn't answer.

She was weary. She looked at the clock. It was 02.58. She left her bedside light on and lay her head back on the pillow. Poor Jackson. He thought he was the only one who had suffered.

He didn't know about her ghost and she wasn't going to tell him.

FOURTEEN
Year Eleven

Hannah told her that Jackson took the break-up badly. He got angry and stormed off in a huff. She said she'd hardly had time to blink when he turned and walked out of her house.

Ali was surprised. At first she'd thought it was because he'd found out about Daniel, but Hannah said she hadn't told him. She'd just said she was fed up and wanted to finish it.

Hannah told her all this at the hairdresser's on Thursday morning.

"I'm just glad I've got it off my chest. Jackson was nice, but we argued a lot."

"And Daniel?"

Hannah was sitting next to Ali in the waiting area. The hairdresser's was busy, a couple of women alongside them, already in gowns, flicking through magazines and glancing at their watches. There was low music playing and, in the corner, on the wall, was a television set showing one of the morning chat shows.

"I know you don't get it about me and Dan. I did feel sorry for him. You know, it was like a challenge to get him – you know – *happy* again. And then I got to like him. He's funny and he likes the same bands as me and we've been watching old DVDs on his laptop. He's less intense than Jackson."

Ali couldn't see it.

"And I'm trying to help him get confidence in himself. Trying to get him to stand up for himself a bit more."

"So is Stephen."

"Stephen's done a lot for him. He thinks Stephen has saved his life."

But Ali knew that it was Jackson who had *really* saved his life. If Jackson hadn't been there when he jumped, he would most certainly have died.

"Are you going to his dad's wedding on Saturday?" Ali said, remembering the invitation that Stephen had had on his bedside table.

Hannah shook her head. "Mum and me are going to this hair conference in Manchester tomorrow? It's been booked for ages. Mum's competing in one of the categories. We won't get back on Saturday until about ten. Thing is, I'm quite glad. Weddings can be a real bore, and I don't want everyone saying, *Oh, look, there's Daniel's new girlfriend*. I'd rather keep a low profile."

Ali nodded. "I broke up with Stephen on Monday."

Hannah nodded. "Well, that was on the cards. How did he take it?"

"He was upset," she said.

Stephen had been surprised when she told him. At first he'd shrugged and managed a smile. She'd felt relieved that he wasn't going to make a scene there in the street. She'd said *sorry* a few times and stood awkwardly on the pavement as passers-by went round or pushed between them.

"I better go," she said.

She turned to walk away and felt his hand on her arm.

"I don't get it. I thought we were OK."

She shrugged, not wanting to get into a conversation. They *were* OK. That was the problem. Being involved with someone was about more than just being OK.

"I'm sorry," she said.

"But we could talk about it."

She shook her head. She saw her bus coming up the road and she wanted to get on it.

"You could come round my house later," he said.

He was holding on to his nametag, pushing it against his tie.

"I'm sorry, Stephen. I just don't want to."

She walked off briskly, heading for the bus stop. All the while she was tense, in case she felt his hand on her arm again. At the stop she waited until some other people got on. She showed her pass and went and sat in a seat. Only when the bus started moving did she turn her head and look towards the building society.

He was standing staring at her as the bus pulled away.

That night he sent her three texts asking her to meet, to call him, to think about it. She didn't send any replies.

"Did you tell him about this?" Hannah said.

Hannah was pointing at her wrist. She hadn't worn the leather band today, but Hannah was acting as though it was there on her arm.

"How do you mean?" Ali said, moving over in the seat as another customer sat down and joined those waiting.

"I've got eyes, Ali. I can sense when something's happening under my nose."

"Nothing happened!" Ali said.

"But you'd like something to happen. Right?"

Ali didn't answer.

"You know what? You might be going to Cambridge University and I might be working in a hairdresser's, but I'm not stupid. You want Jackson. You have him. Let's face it, him and me weren't going anywhere."

Hannah's mum appeared. She was looking harassed and holding a black brush that was coated with hair dye.

"Hannah, can you come help me with a colour?"

"Better go."

Ali stood up.

"See you around."

Hannah went off after her mum. Ali walked out of the shop feeling odd. She and Hannah had been in the same form class for five years and over the past weeks they had made a sort of connection. Now that was gone. Ali would probably only see her in passing. A familiar face, someone she used to know. Maybe she'd go into the hairdresser's for a cut and Hannah would do it and she'd leave a tip and after she left Hannah would say to someone, *I used to go to school with her. Bit of a boffin type.*

Later that night she built up enough courage to ring Jackson. The call went to voicemail so she left a message. "So sorry to hear about you and Hannah. I had no idea anything was up. Especially after we were having that conversation last week. What a coincidence, though. I broke up with Stephen a couple of days ago. You remember we talked about it? Anyway, I'm around if you fancy having a chat. If you want to talk it over. Just give me a ring or send me a text or something."

By Friday afternoon she hadn't had a reply. She decided to go and see him, friend to friend. She stood in the shower for a while and put newly ironed clothes on. She took the leather band out of her drawer and fastened it. She left home and walked up her street, passing by Stephen's car. It looked like it had just been cleaned. It was gleaming, and the inside was tidy and neat as ever. On the dashboard she saw Stephen's dark glasses case. For a second she felt something. A stab of regret that things hadn't turned out quite the way she'd thought they would when she had first fancied Stephen. He had seemed so interesting, his scar suggesting a wild streak, someone who hit out first and thought about it later. When he put his dark glasses on and got into the car, she'd felt special. How wrong she had been.

Then she thought of Jackson and felt a spurt of anticipation. What would she say when she saw him? *I was checking you were all right. I'm so sorry to hear about you and Hannah. Do you fancy a chat?* They could sit on the sofa in his loft room and she could listen sympathetically to everything he said. Maybe he would get a drink or maybe he would say, *Let's get a couple of cans of beer and go up to Blackwood.* Just to be with him for a while. That was the thing. Once Hannah was out of his head, then she would be around. It wouldn't take much of an adjustment. Hadn't he been giving her signals for weeks? Hadn't he been touching her, catching her eye? Hadn't he given her a gift?

She rang Jackson's bell but there was no answer. She was instantly irritated. She wondered where he was. She walked in the direction of school. There was a small chance that he might be there. In any case, she had nothing else to do. She felt her anxiety build up as she turned into the school road. This would look natural. She was going into school for something; to see the careers woman again or to pop in and see her old form teacher to check whether she'd given in her envelope for the GCSE results. If she bumped into him, well and good. If not, she'd go home.

He came out of the gate as she was approaching it. He was wearing shorts and carrying a sports bag and racquet case with him. He was drinking from a bottle of water. With him were a couple of other kids from their class. They were laughing loudly and one of them noticed her before Jackson did.

"Hi," she said, when they stopped. "What you up to?"

"Duh?"

Two of them held up their badminton racquets.

"Course," she said, feeling stupid.

"I wanted to have a word with you," she said to Jackson, glancing awkwardly at the other lads.

"What's up?" he said.

The other two boys walked on, making suggestive noises. She gave them an impatient look and tutted and rolled her eyes at Jackson.

"Are you OK?"

"Yeah."

"I mean, are you *really* all right?" she said, sidestepping a bunch of younger kids who were tumbling out of the school gates.

He laughed. "What, you mean about me and Hannah breaking up?"

She nodded.

"Oh, you know. No one likes to be dumped. But I'll get by."

"She said you were upset."

He shrugged.

"You know me and Stephen broke up?"

"You said in your message. That's good. It was what you wanted."

"How did it go in Brighton?" she said.

"Good. We did a lot of work. I'll be going down there a lot more this summer."

"Oh."

She gave a smile, trying to cover up a growing feeling of frustration. She heard the gentle tooting of a car horn and saw one of the teacher's cars coming out of the gates, groups of students moving slowly to the side to let it pass. He was going to be away for most of the summer. She tried to think of something to say but couldn't. It hadn't gone as she'd wanted it to. From behind she could hear the other lads talking, laughing and joking. Jackson looked at her and frowned.

"You all right?"

"Yes. I must go. I've a couple of things to sort out in school."

"See you, then."

He walked off. She turned to watch him go. After a few seconds he turned out of the school road and disappeared. She closed her eyes with anguish. On Monday it had been Stephen watching her go. Now she was watching Jackson go.

She waited a while and then walked away from school, feeling her throat tighten. She got to her front door just as her mum's car pulled up. Her mum honked her horn but Ali didn't look, didn't wave. She just thrust her key into the lock and surged into the house, running upstairs and closing her room door.

What had been the point of it all? In the last few weeks she had been swept away with thoughts about Jackson. In every look, in every touch, she had felt a whispered promise, and now he was acting as though she were just another kid in the class, no one special.

She flopped down on her bed, pulled the leather band off her arm and chucked it to the side, watching as it missed her bedside table and half dropped, half floated on to the carpet.

On Saturday, during the afternoon, she looked out of her mum's bedroom window. Stephen's car wasn't there. She wondered if he'd gone to Daniel's father's wedding. She remembered the invite. The silver balloons and the gold lettering: *The Rainham Hotel, Saturday 19th June 4.30.* Stephen had laughed it off, but now that he was on his own, might he not go along? Stephen really liked Daniel, really liked helping him and being a part of his life. Would he feel the same, she wondered, if he knew that Daniel was together with Hannah? Would Daniel be so bothered about Stephen and Jonesy now that he had Hannah?

Everything had changed. Wasn't that what she'd wanted? She'd been fed up with the four of them going out together, fed up with their car rides, their trips to nowhere. Now that was all finished. Hannah had Daniel. Stephen still had Jonesy. She had no one. Jackson might as well have stayed in Brighton.

She went downstairs about six. Her dad was sleeping on the sofa and her mum was reading a book.

"We'll be out late tonight," her mum said. "Will you be all right on your own?"

"How come?"

"One of Dad's colleagues is having a leaving party."

"Right."

"You could come if you wanted! They've got a teenage son, I think."

"No!"

"It was just a thought. Are you working in the shop next week?"

"Monday and Wednesday."

"Mrs Lumsden's got a nice grandson. Tom, his name is."

She didn't answer. A car horn sounded from out in the street.

"You're not pining for that Stephen, are you?"

"No!" she said. "It was me who dumped him!"

"Well, what with your studies. It's probably all for the best."

She closed her eyes.

"What?" her dad said, waking up suddenly and looking round the room. "What's happening?"

"Nothing, Dad," she said, and walked upstairs.

She had to get Jackson's attention. She'd thought he'd liked her. She'd thought that for weeks. He wasn't heartbroken over Hannah, but he didn't seem in a hurry to move on. She needed him to notice her, to want to be with her even if it was only as a friend. In that way they could begin to bond, begin to hook up with each other. She *had* to pull him towards her; otherwise he'd be off to Brighton on the first train and she wouldn't see him all summer.

She walked up and down in her room. It was nine o'clock. Why hadn't he called her? Or sent a text? She was alone. He was alone. It made sense for them to be together. She sat down and picked up her mobile. She was going to ring him again. She was going to make him *see* her.

He answered immediately. She felt good. He'd taken her call when he could have let it go to voicemail.

"Hi," she said.

"I was going to ring you tomorrow. . ." he started.

"There was something I wanted to tell you, but I wasn't sure whether to or not."

"I thought you sounded a bit funny the other day."

"Did you know that Hannah and Daniel are together?"

There was silence.

"I don't think it's been going on very long. Just a week or so, but I thought you should know."

"How do you know this?"

"I saw them together and then Hannah told me."

"Why didn't she tell me?"

"I don't know."

"Together. With Daniel?"

"Yeah."

"I should go."

"You're not upset that I told you?"

"No. I'll give you a call later."

"Come over if you want."

"I can't. There's something I've got to do. I'll come and see you tomorrow."

The call ended and Ali lowered her mobile. She finally had Jackson's attention. *I'll come and see you tomorrow.* That was a good start.

FIFTEEN

The front doorbell rang just after ten-thirty. Ali was lying in the dark of her room thinking about the phone call she had had with Jackson. She'd been there for a long time. She'd been going back over what she'd said and wondering whether it had been a good idea and whether or not Jackson would be more interested in her because she'd said it.

The bell interrupted her thoughts. She sat up as it rang again in a short burst, as though someone had jabbed it impatiently. She stood up, feeling a little dazed, and turned the light on. It made her blink, and she smoothed her clothes down as the bell rang again.

Could it be Jackson?

Had he come round to see her?

She pushed her feet into her sandals and pulled a brush through her hair and walked quickly down the stairs. At the front door she paused and took a breath.

Stephen was standing on her step.

She frowned. "What's up?" she said.

"Can I come in?"

She stood back and he walked in. Her heart sank. Had he come to try to persuade her to go back with him?

"I've got Jackson in the car. He's in a temper. He wants me to

107

take him to Daniel's dad's wedding. He says you told him that Daniel and Hannah were together? I don't get it. I saw Daniel last night. I took him to boxing. He never said anything to me. *What* is this about Daniel and Hannah?"

Stephen was talking *at* her. It annoyed her, but she was more put out by the fact that Jackson was outside, in the car. He had gone to Stephen when he could have come to her.

"Hannah and Daniel are together," she said. "Hannah got close to Daniel. Daniel got close to Hannah. What else is there to say?"

"When?"

In the tiny hallway, Stephen seemed to tower above her.

"Last week. Did you say Jackson was in your car?" she said, looking towards the door.

Stephen nodded. He looked perplexed. He looked mildly hurt.

"I saw Daniel last night," he whispered. "He never said a word."

Ali was exasperated. "Why should he *say* anything to you?" she cried.

Stephen pulled his lips across his teeth. His scar looked redder, deeper.

"You need to come with us," he said. "Help me calm Jackson down. He wants to confront Daniel and Hannah. He wants me to take him to the wedding."

"Hannah's not at the wedding," Ali said. "Hannah's away with her mum in Manchester. Why does he want to see them? I thought he wasn't *bothered* about Hannah. He told me he wasn't broken-hearted!"

"You don't get it, Ali. It's a boy thing. It's not about feelings. It's about honour."

"Honour?" she huffed. "What is this, *The Three Musketeers*?"

"Come out to the car. See if you can talk him out of it. I've tried, but he says he'll get a minicab if I don't take him."

She hesitated. This was nothing to do with her. Jackson had made that clear by going to Stephen. Why should she get involved?

"He'll make a show of himself at Daniel's dad's wedding."

Why hadn't Jackson just come to her? She could have calmed him down. Wasn't that the exact reason that she had told him about Hannah and Daniel? Why did he have to get Stephen involved?

"I don't know. It's late. . ."

"Come on. I'm just trying to stop him making a fool of himself. If he comes over all heavy at the wedding, Daniel's dad and his family might get involved."

She plucked her keys off the hall table. All the while she was wondering why she was bothered. To her it had been simple. She cared for Jackson. She thought he cared for her. Now he was only fired up by some sense of being slighted by Daniel and Hannah.

"Come on! I'm worried he'll storm off and go on his own."

Jackson was standing on the road outside the car. He was leaning on the roof with his hands, his arms out straight, rigid.

She went straight up to him. "Why are you so upset? I don't get it. I thought you said you were all right? I would never have told you if I thought you were upset about breaking up with Hannah."

He didn't answer, just shook his head. His face was flat and she couldn't see any expression in it.

"Do you want to get back with her?"

He shook his head.

"Well. . ." She stood hopelessly.

"Are we going?" Jackson said to Stephen. "Because I can walk down to the station and pick up a cab."

Stephen opened the driver's door and Jackson got in the passenger seat. Ali opened the back and got in.

"Wait, don't start the car yet," she said. "What is the point of this?"

"I have to face him. I have to *show* myself. I don't want him to think that I know and I'm not going to do anything about it."

"But what does it matter! You don't want to get back with her. . ."

"It matters, Ali," Stephen said. "A few weeks ago we saved this kid's life. . ."

"That's all you ever go on about! What does it matter if we saved his life? You said you wanted him to be *happy*. He is happy. He likes Hannah. She likes him. So what!"

"It's about respect," Jackson said quietly. "I stopped him from choking to death. I did. *Me*."

He said *me* in a tone of voice that seemed to challenge them to disagree with him.

"The first chance he gets, he goes with my girlfriend. It's not about me and Hannah. It's about *respect*. He did not respect me and I want him to know that I'm angry."

"Why not let me and Jonesy deal with it?" Stephen said. "First thing tomorrow morning we'll go round and see him. We'll have it out with him. He had no right to treat you like that."

"Stephen, this is for me to deal with. Not you, not Jonesy. Me. I need to face up to him and Hannah and tell them what I think."

"Hannah's not there. She's in Manchester with her mum," Ali said.

"I don't care. Then I'll face up to him. Now, tonight. This is not the sort of thing you put off. You do something about it as soon as you know. That's what you do. That's what respect is about."

"It'll spoil his dad's wedding reception."

"It won't. When we get there, you go in and tell him I want to talk to him. You get him to come outside and I'll have it out with him there."

"Why don't we do it somewhere else? Why not meet him in some neutral place?" Stephen said.

"What am I going to do? Phone him up and say *Meet me at McDonald's so I can give you a pasting*?"

"A pasting? I thought you just wanted to talk to him," Ali said.

"I don't know what I'm going to do. I just know that if we don't move off from here then I'm going to get out and get a cab and do it anyway!"

Stephen started the engine. The car pulled away from the kerb and they drove along in a thick silence for a while. Up ahead was the A13, and Stephen moved on to it. After a while the lights of the Ford factory glittered from one side of the dual carriageway. The windscreen wipers were going, even though Ali couldn't see the rain falling. The traffic was sparse, just a lorry on the inside lane that seemed to be standing still as they whipped past, its lights receding into the distance. Ali wanted to put her hand out and touch Jackson's shoulder, but she didn't. He was all sharp edges, the top of his arm rigid, his elbow stiff. She sensed a hardness from him that she'd not felt before. She'd seen him get angry, that day in the motorway services and other times when lads had looked at Hannah, but it soon passed and he was relaxed and was often sheepish about his outburst. Now he seemed full up with something: jealousy? Anger? Hurt feelings?

Up ahead she saw the sign for Harry's Diner. It was still on, still flickering lightly even though the café was closed at weekends. It was just a siren light drawing cars and lorries to a closed café. The click of the indicator sounded. Stephen was slowing down, moving off the dual carriageway towards Harry's Diner. Ali was puzzled.

"What's going on?" Jackson said, a hint of nastiness in his voice.

The car came to a halt in the parking area for the diner. Ali looked out of the window. Behind the café, it was complete darkness.

"What's this place?" Jackson said, looking around.

"This wedding is in the Rainham Hotel," Stephen said. "It's about five or so minutes from here, out by the marshes. You stay here; Ali and me'll go to the wedding and pull Daniel out. We'll make up some story to get him into the car and bring him back here. Then you can talk to him. We can all talk to him. Then we can all go home."

Ali stared rigidly out at the passing cars. She didn't trust herself to speak. Stephen was so keen to be involved in this story. It was nothing to do with him, but he wanted to be part of it.

"What am I supposed to do here?" Jackson said. "I don't even know where I am."

"Calm down? Chill out? We can be back here in fifteen minutes, tops."

"This is not what we agreed."

"You got no choice. I'm not taking you to muck up his dad's wedding. And I don't want his family ganging up on you."

"I'll ring for a cab."

"It's gone eleven. You'll wait ages for a cab at this time on a Saturday night. Why not just let us go and get him? I won't let you down. If he's there, I'll get him and bring him here."

"It's raining."

"Stand under the café awning."

Ali couldn't see Jackson's face. She heard him swear quietly; then the door opened and he got out. Stephen hardly waited for the door to shut before he pulled back into the traffic again.

"I don't get it," she said.

"Give him a chance to chill."

"Are we going for Daniel?"

"Yeah, course. But the two of them talking there? It's likely to be less trouble than in this wedding. And I'll be there to referee things."

Ali rolled her eyes. Stephen was picturing himself as the older, wiser person. Like Jonesy.

He drove on carefully, staring forward, his hand hovering over the gear stick. Up ahead was the Queen Elizabeth Bridge. Soon they took the slip road down towards the marshes. Once they were on the minor road, Stephen slowed down and began to speak, to give her instructions. They passed a sign that said *RAINHAM HOTEL: Parties, Weddings, Dinners 400 yards.*

"You go into the reception. I'll sit in the car. Say Hannah wants to see him or something."

"But what if he's been in touch with Hannah?"

"Ask him. If he has, then say something different. Just get him to come out of the reception and into the car."

She sat still, feeling annoyed at herself for having been dragged into it. Here she was in the car with *Stephen*. Not even with Jackson. And now she had to go into Daniel's father's wedding reception and look for him and tempt him out and into the car.

"Look!" Stephen said, sharply.

There was a figure walking along in the distance.

"It's Daniel," he said.

"No, it's not."

It was someone in a suit and Ali looked hard until she realized that it *was* Daniel. His short hair and formal dress had thrown her. He was alone, walking away from the Rainham Hotel and the wedding. Stephen put his indicator on and the car came to a halt.

"Get out. Ask him about Hannah and then get him to come into the car."

Ali opened the door when they were still a couple of car lengths away from him.

"Hiya," she called and Daniel looked up, surprised to see her.

"What you doing here?"

"Well, we were invited," she said.

"It's all over now."

It was drizzling. In the street light the rain shone.

"You heard from Hannah?" she said.

He shook his head. "She's on her way back from Manchester. In any case, my mobile's dead."

"She called me. We're going past her place. Do you want a lift?"

"Did she tell you to come and get me?"

"Yes."

"I thought you two were finished," he said, pointing to Stephen.

"But we're still mates."

Daniel nodded and walked towards the car.

"Hiya, mate," he said to Stephen.

"All right?"

Daniel got in the back. Ali got in the passenger seat.

"You've saved my life, you two. The cabs were all taken and I absolutely had to get away from my relatives. Plus it's raining."

Stephen didn't answer. He went back up the slip road on to the A13 and put his foot down. Ali felt the car pull away and shoot off down the outside lane.

SIXTEEN

"Where are we going?" Daniel said when they went round a roundabout and started to go back down the other side of the A13.

"I've just got to do something," Stephen said.

Ali stared straight ahead. Moments before, they'd passed Harry's Diner, but because they were on the wrong side of the dual carriageway, they couldn't turn back into it. It meant going a mile or so up the road and coming back. She'd looked out of the window to see if she could see Jackson standing waiting for them, but he wasn't anywhere. When they finally pulled into the forecourt of the café she still couldn't see him.

"What's up?" Daniel said.

Ali could feel a change in the atmosphere of the car, as though Daniel was sensing something.

Stephen paused, looking around. Then he turned towards the back of the old car park, moving slowly, avoiding the holes in the tarmac the way he always did. The headlights of the car swept across the waste ground, the disused petrol pumps, the wire fencing, the old vans that had been parked there and were never moved. As they swung round, the headlights illuminated the old container, and there, standing beside it, was Jackson.

"What?"

"We need to sort something out," Stephen said. "Jackson wants to see you."

"You brought me here to see him?"

"Just to clear the air," Ali said.

"Why didn't you just say that Jackson wanted to see me?"

It occurred to Ali then that Jackson had been the one person who Daniel hadn't seen since the night up at Blackwood.

When the car stopped, Daniel got out, looking around uncertainly. Jackson walked straight across to him. When he got closer, he seemed to falter, thrown by Daniel's suit and his haircut. The headlights of the car threw out a block of yellow light. The fine rain seemed to hang in it.

"What's up, mate?" Daniel said, looking apprehensive.

Jackson didn't say a word. With both hands he gave Daniel a powerful push that made him stumble backwards.

Stephen was out of the car in seconds and ran round to hold Jackson back. Daniel stood up uncertainly. The sign that said *Harry's Diner* seemed a long way away, as did the A13, the cars only distant shapes whizzing past. The space they were in was quiet, as if it were in some kind of bubble. Even though it was raining, it felt hot. Ali felt uncomfortable and there was a gnawing unease inside her. She didn't like this.

"I thought we were just having a talk?" she said, weakly.

They stood in a small knot at the edge of the headlights.

"OK, let's talk," Jackson said. "How come you went with my girlfriend behind my back?"

Daniel stuttered something and Ali felt a sting of pity. He

glanced around, looking over towards the road and the cars rushing past. He must have wondered where he was. A black hole in the middle of Dagenham.

"How come?" Jackson said, his voice louder.

"Let him speak," Ali said. "I thought you were going to let him speak."

"You and Hannah were finished. That's how it seemed. I haven't got anything else to say. I'm sorry, mate; if I thought you'd be upset about it, I wouldn't have..."

"That's crap. She was with me and you knew it."

"I never saw you together. She came round to see me, almost every day. I just thought that you were over."

"You should have spoken to Jackson," Stephen said, his voice low and steady, as if he was deliberately trying to calm things. "You knew they were a couple. They were in your class at school."

"What is this, Stephen? I've done nothing against you," Daniel said. "Why did *you* bring me here?"

"You don't crap on your mates, Dan. Hannah was Jackson's girl."

"But you weren't close, though. Be honest, Jackson," Ali said.

Someone had to state the truth. She knew it, and Jackson, if he was honest, knew it too. Never mind that he had teased Ali for weeks, made her think he wanted her. He and Hannah had been fed up with each other for a long time.

Jackson ignored her. He stared at Daniel.

"Hannah said you hadn't seen much of her. She said you were finished and it was only a matter of time."

"It isn't about *Hannah*. It's about respect. You had no respect for me!"

"*Respect?*"

"Jackson's right," Stephen joined in. "You should have shown him some respect."

"What it is with you? One minute you're telling me to stand up to bullies and here you are ganging up against me?"

"I'm not taking this," Jackson said, stepping closer to Daniel. "I'm not having him wriggle out of this."

Ali got in between them.

"Let's go, Jackson," she said, softly, touching his arm. "You've said your bit. Let's go home."

Jackson hesitated. Then all of a sudden he looked deflated. As if it hadn't turned out the way he'd hoped. It was just an argument, a damp squib.

"Let's leave it," Stephen said, and started to walk round the front of the car.

Jackson swore under his breath as Ali edged him away by the arm.

Daniel turned and walked towards the car. "Maybe if you'd treated her better, she might still be with you," he said.

Jackson spun round. He shook off Ali's hand.

"What?"

He lifted his arm and smashed it into Daniel's back. With his other hand he grabbed Daniel's suit jacket and pulled him backwards until he was flat on the ground.

"Stop it!" Stephen shouted, hurrying back.

Stephen pulled Jackson away and Jackson let go of Daniel. Stephen took hold of him and walked him backwards out of the headlights until they were up against the container. He held Jackson in an armlock.

"You've made your point!"

"Please, Jackson, leave it," Ali said. "Let's go."

Jackson shook Stephen off and stood still. He seemed to be calming himself. He took deep breaths. Ali helped Daniel up off the ground. She brushed his jacket. She straightened his sleeve and felt his arm trembling.

"It's all right," she whispered. "He's got it out of his system."

Daniel shook her away.

"We'll go," Jackson said, moments later, walking back towards the car, "but he's not coming."

"How do you mean?" Stephen said.

"He's not coming in the car."

"How's he going to get home?"

"He can walk."

"Don't be stupid," Daniel said, a hint of annoyance in his voice. "I can't walk home from here. I don't even know where I am."

"Ring for a cab."

"My mobile's dead."

"You could use mine," Ali said, pulling hers out of her jacket pocket.

"I don't want to ring for a cab," Daniel said, a slight tremor in his voice.

"I'm not having him in the car," Jackson said, his anger brewing again.

"Let's just get in the car," Ali said, getting cross, feeling annoyed that she'd been dragged out on this stupid errand. She opened the back door, causing the inside light to come on.

120

"We can sort something out," Stephen said.

"He's not getting in the car," Jackson said.

"Grow up!"

Daniel said it loudly and made an impatient gesture at Jackson, then walked towards the open car door, but Jackson grabbed his shoulder and twisted him round.

"I SAVED YOUR LIFE!" he said. "AND YOU PISSED ALL OVER ME!"

Ali watched as Daniel seemed to rise up and face Jackson. With both hands he shoved Jackson in the chest. Jackson stumbled back and Daniel turned to the car and was about to get in when he was grabbed from behind. Jackson took his arm and swung him away from the car. Daniel tried to pull his arm out of Jackson's hold. They went back and forward until Jackson seemed to throw Daniel away from the car and he gathered speed and shot across the tarmac until he collided with the corner of the old container. There was a dull thump and Daniel stopped instantly and slid down the edge and on to the ground.

The rain fell harder.

A dog barked in the distance. Two, three times, then it stopped.

The three of them stood looking at Daniel. Ali was the first to take a step forward.

"Are you all right, Daniel?"

"Dan? You OK?" Stephen said.

Jackson said nothing. Ali walked towards Daniel, a feeling of dread in her ribs.

"Daniel? What's up, mate? Did you knock your head?"

He was lying slumped over, just outside the headlights of the car. Ali couldn't see his face, just the top of his head. She found herself looking away from him, staring at the side of the old container: the ribbed metal, the rusted patches, like flaking skin.

She knelt down beside him.

"Probably best to sit up," she said with a half laugh.

She put one hand behind his head and the other under his chin and tried to help him sit up. It wasn't easy. His head felt so heavy. She looked at the others. The headlights were behind them, so their faces were in the dark. Stephen had one hand on his forehead and he was swearing over and over again. Jackson was just staring ahead, his eyes looking like two black holes.

"Come on, Daniel," she said. "Try and sit up."

She took her hand away from the back of his head. It felt wet. When she looked it was black. She stood up and stepped back, away from Daniel, moving the palm of her hand so that it was lit up by the headlights.

It wasn't black. It was red. Blood red.

SEVENTEEN
Year Thirteen

It was Alison's night to look after her gran. She'd been at the house for a couple of hours. Her gran's carer had been and gone and now they were sitting watching the television quietly together.

"Is Bel coming?" her gran said.

"Bel's already been this evening," Alison said. "She gave you your tea. Chicken pie and mash."

"Chicken pie and mash. I like that."

Gran's dog, Rex, was on her knee, curled up in a horseshoe. Gran's hand stroked Rex's head in a rhythmic way. Alison noticed, not for the first time, that the third finger of Gran's left hand was weighted down with rings: wedding, engagement and eternity. Gran wore them all the time. She hadn't taken them off for many years and they had become a physical part of her. *You can have my jewellery when I die*, Gran used to say. She said it when her mind was still there; when she could still see her life travelling forward towards a day when she would no longer be around. Now every day was the same for Gran: every day was static, it didn't lead on from the day before; neither did it lead anywhere else. Gran lived in a kind of

Groundhog Day world. The carers came, the carers went. Rex was there, the meals were provided, the telly went on, the telly went off, Gran got up, Gran went to bed.

Alison wasn't upset by these thoughts. Things had been like this for a long time. She was used to it. The whole family had become accustomed to this world that Gran inhabited.

She looked at her college bag sitting by the door, where she had dropped it when she came in. It was bulging. She needed to clear it out, but there never seemed to be time. That day she'd been on the go since early morning. She'd had a run; three kilometres around the streets. She'd got into college early and done some work in the library before her revision classes. At lunch time she did some work in the careers office, something she had volunteered to do months before. It was good for the CV, people said, but she did it because it took up time and kept her busy. In the afternoon she wrote a couple of timed essays in the library with some girls from one of her classes. They policed each other, making sure that no one cheated. The girls had gone off afterwards to the local shopping centre for a coffee. They'd asked her to go, but she'd said she had other things to do – which was true in a way, but not her main reason for not going. When she got home from school, her dad was in, and she got changed and helped him clear the garage for a car boot sale he was planning to do the following weekend.

Then she came to Gran's.

She had missed something out. The letter. The one that

had been on the hall table when she got home from college. She'd read it quickly and then put it in her bag and got on with helping her dad. Now she looked at her bag and pictured the envelope inside, sandwiched between one of her many handouts or past papers or the sheaves of notes she was making in preparation for her exams. She got up and pulled her bag across to the settee. She took the envelope out and unfolded the letter.

"Have you got a letter, Alison?" her gran said.

Alison nodded.

"I used to get letters from my sister. You know Deborah? Who emigrated to Australia? I think I got one the other day."

Alison just smiled. Deborah had been dead for over ten years.

She unfolded the paper. There was no address, just *Dear Ali* at the top. She read it again.

I've probably given you and Stephen a real shock. I know Stephen thinks he will get all the blame, but I won't let that happen. I will make sure I tell the whole story. I will make sure that my part in it is fully explained. No one meant for this to happen, but somehow we did make it happen.

In Brighton I tried to live with what happened. I've kept busy. Sometimes a day or two might go by and I wouldn't think of it. But then it comes back. It's like this crushing weight I carry round.

I went into a church once. I sat down and felt this calm come over me. The place was so still, so quiet. I sat in this

125

wooden pew and I felt like I wanted to kneel down and ask for forgiveness. But I don't believe in God, so I've got to ask someone else for forgiveness.

Do you see?

I would love to talk to you. To see you. Could you manage that? I'll come to your college tomorrow afternoon? About four?

That's if you want to see me again. After everything. J x

Jackson was going to go to the police. He was going to tell them everything about that night two years before. It made her feel light-headed with worry. That's why she had folded it up and put it away. Out of sight, out of mind.

The programme had ended and Gran was looking at her.

"My sister sent me letters all the way from Australia. They took weeks to come. I used to look forward to them and I used to save the stamps for a charity. We had a whole jar of stamps, packed up to the top."

"That's good, Gran," Alison said.

Her gran remembered things from thirty, forty, even fifty years ago. Small details, tiny insignificant things that had somehow stayed in her mind: the name of a café she had used, Lyons Corner House; a particular type of make-up she'd bought, Max Factor Panstick; or the shade of a pair of tights, American Tan. These things were there, in her head, instantly. But talking about Bel, the carer, or the day of the week, or the season of the year, these were things she couldn't do. Parts of her memory had simply shrivelled up like a few wilted blooms in a vase of flowers.

Sometimes she envied her gran.

Whole bits of her life that had faded away.

Alison wished she could do that. If her memories would fade and disintegrate, then it would be as if those things had never even happened. She could wake up in the morning without a clamp across her chest; she could think about the day ahead without a shadow dimming her view, darkening her sights, taking the light from her life.

If she could just erase her memories.

"Is Bel coming?" Gran said.

"No, Bel's already been tonight. You had chicken pie and mash for dinner. Remember?"

"Lovely. Chicken pie. That's my favourite."

Later, while she was waiting for her dad to pick her up, she tidied out her bag. She threw away a lot of stuff and filed her handouts away. At the bottom of her bag she found some downloaded pages on Downing College, Cambridge, where she was due to go in September. She looked at the pictures of students walking up a wide gravel path, smiling and laughing. Beyond them was a grey building with long windows and heavy wooden doors. There were giant trees at the edge of the photos. She would be an undergraduate studying English. She would have her own room in halls and be in charge of her grant and her bank account. She would have meals in the dining room and would only have to go off-site if she wanted to. She would make new friends and have a different life. The people she would meet would only know her as eighteen-year-old Alison Rose, three As and a B (or maybe four As). She would be starting fresh, a new bit of her life.

She longed for it. She ached for it.

But would it happen if Jackson went to the police?

She replaced the sheets and tidied out the zippered sections at the front of her bag. There were tissues and memory sticks and half-empty packets of mints. She pushed her fingers into the last section at the bottom, one that she never used. She half expected it to be empty, but it wasn't.

She pulled out the leather band that Jackson had once given her. She hadn't worn it for almost two years. She looked at it for a long time; then she slipped it over her wrist and fastened the loop over the button.

She liked the way it looked. She had always liked it.

EIGHTEEN

Year Eleven

Daniel did not move.

The drizzle was hanging in the air. Ali felt the dampness on her face and on her lips. When she looked around, she saw it in the headlights of the car like a fine spray. No one moved. It seemed like the three of them were waiting for Daniel to *do* something. They stood completely still, staring at the container, at the boy on the ground.

"Daniel?" Ali said.

Stephen moved. He walked forward and squatted down beside Daniel. Ali joined him, standing above them. Only Jackson stayed back, rigid, by the car, staring at them.

"You all right, Dan?"

There was no answer. Not a sound.

Ali felt her insides turning to liquid. Her hand was sticky with blood and she didn't know what to do with it. She wiped it down one leg of her jeans. She rubbed the skin until it felt dry. She didn't look at it again, just let it hang by her side.

"Daniel, mate, it was just a push, just an accident. You've hit your head, that's all," Stephen said.

There was no sign that he'd heard. He was still. He was quiet.

He looked floppy, like a soft toy that had been thrown across a room by a child.

"Shall we move him?" Ali said, her voice squeaking with dryness. "Lay him on his side? I don't know – give him the kiss of life?"

"I don't think he's breathing."

Stephen had his fingers on Daniel's neck. Then he picked up his hand and felt around his wrist. Ali was waiting for him to look at the back of Daniel's head, but he did not.

"Are you sure? How can you be sure? What about his head?"

"He's probably in shock," Jackson said, finally speaking, stepping towards them. "Come on, Stephen. You know first aid."

Jackson's moving figure cut across the headlights of the car. He cast a momentary shadow; then he was there beside Ali. He was inches away from her but she didn't reach out to touch him. She felt separated from him, as though there were a sheet of glass between them.

She looked helplessly towards the road. The shape of the café was outlined against the lights of the A13. Above it, like a scruffy flagpole, was the flickering neon light that said *Harry's Diner*. In between was the pitted tarmac of the old car park. In the darkness it looked like black water, a deep lake that they had to cross.

A siren sounded from the road beyond, and Ali saw the flash of blue as a police car sped along the far side. It was followed by another, seconds later.

"I'm calling an ambulance," she said.

She pulled her phone out of her pocket and flicked it open.

"Wait, wait. Don't do that," Stephen said.

"Why?" Ali hissed.

"There's no point in calling an ambulance if there's nothing they can do!"

"But they will. They'll know what to do."

Stephen stood up. He stepped across to the old container. He was running his hand up and down the edge. The ugly metal structure sat immovable. How long had it been there? A year? Five years? It had been forgotten about, left to rust and crumble, rooted to the spot in a car park that had been deserted a long time before.

Jackson stepped forward and knelt down beside Daniel.

"Come on," he whispered, shaking Daniel by the shoulder.

"Look at the back of his head," Ali said, a lump forming in her throat.

Jackson did not look at the back of Daniel's head.

Screeching brakes sounded from the road. They all looked round. It was a lorry that had come to a sudden halt just outside Harry's Diner. Just behind it was a throb of blue, colouring the side of the stationary lorry, going on and off, making the flickering neon sign look feeble.

"It's the *law*," Stephen said.

He stepped towards the car door, leaned in and turned the headlights off. The area plunged into blackness. Ali felt weak in her legs, her hands wanting to reach out for something to hold on to. She made herself breathe slowly. It would be all right. Her eyes would adjust. She would be able to see things in a moment.

"Don't move, don't say a word."

"We should call an ambulance," she whispered.

"It's too late."

She put the flat of her hand over her mouth as the blue flashing light seemed to be suddenly brighter, lighting up a bigger area on the other side of the café. Then she realized that it was a second police car parked at the front of the lorry.

"We don't want them here," Stephen whispered.

"They might be able to help!" Ali said, her voice sounding as though it was coming from deep down inside her throat.

"It's too late."

The blue light continued and from where they were, in the dark, they watched as an officer got out of his car and walked along the side of the lorry. He moved up and down slowly. He was partly bent over, as though he was looking at the chassis, at the load that was on the vehicle.

"They might come in here," Jackson said. "We should move out of the way. We don't want them to see us."

Ali's eyes were adjusting to the darkness. She could see across the tarmac. The back of the café was clearer now and she could just make out the weeds and old crates and supermarket trolleys that inhabited the old car park. She turned to the side and looked at Daniel lying in exactly the same position as before.

Stephen was by her side. She hadn't heard him move. He took her elbow and put his finger over his lips. Then Jackson was at her other side. The three of them moved past Daniel's body to the other side of the old container. They turned and stepped round the edge of it. At the back of the container was a gap of about a metre, but Ali had no intention of going there. Weeks before, she and Stephen had stood in this very place. The night that they'd saved Daniel's life. Stephen had been ill, traumatized by what had happened in Blackwood Park.

Now they were hiding from a police car.

They stood still, in a line, Stephen at the front, Ali next, Jackson behind her. She was standing at an odd angle, and apart from the flashing blue light, she couldn't see a thing.

"What are we going to do?"

"I don't know," Stephen said. "I have to think."

"We should get an ambulance!"

"An ambulance is not going to make any difference."

"We should take him to a hospital."

"We'll have to leave him here."

"How can we? We can't just leave him here!"

"What do you suggest? It wasn't me who hurt him!" Stephen whispered, his head twisted back.

"I never meant it. You know I never meant to hurt him."

There was a sound from the lorry and they all tensed. Its engine was starting up. The blue light from the police car in front of it seemed to be flashing on and off further along, moving up the dual carriageway. Ali could see the faintest glow in the sky moving off towards the Queen Elizabeth Bridge. Then the lorry drove out into the traffic. She couldn't actually *see* it go, but she heard the rumble and puff of its engine as it moved off.

That left one police car. After a moment its blue light went off and there was darkness again, only a pink flicker from the neon diner sign.

"Will it drive off?" Jackson whispered.

Ali listened. There was no sound. What was it doing? Sitting waiting for an emergency call? Deciding what to do? Where to go? Stephen edged forward and she looked around his arm. Across the car park she could see the glow from the sidelights of the police car. It was too far away to see what the officers inside were doing. It was even too far to see if there were one or two officers in the car.

"What are they going to do?" Jackson said.

"I don't know!"

The rain got heavier suddenly. She heard it pitter patter on the container and felt actual raindrops on her head. Daniel was still lying on the ground, the rain falling on him.

"We have to do something. We have to take Daniel to a *hospital*," she said, in a harsh whisper. "We can't just leave him there!"

"Let me think! Let me think!" Stephen said.

"He's dead, Ali," Jackson whispered. He was close enough for her to feel his hot breath on the side of her face.

"You can't know that for sure."

"We'll have to explain it. How are we going to explain it?" Stephen said.

"It was an accident. You said it was an accident. They'll understand."

"No, they won't," Stephen said.

"Ssh," Jackson said. "That police car is still there. Do you think they know something? Do they know we're here?"

"It's dark over here. They can't see us."

"If the law finds us here with him, we are in trouble. The worst trouble ever."

"He might just be *unconscious*."

"I couldn't feel a pulse. There were no breath sounds. He must have hit his head; he's cracked his skull. This thing is metal," Stephen said, touching the corner of the container. "He's hit it at speed and his head cracked. I heard the sound. I heard it!"

Ali felt a terrible clawing feeling inside her chest. She stood very still and knew that she was beginning to shake. She hiccupped a couple of sobs and Jackson put his hand on her shoulder.

"It was an accident, Ali," he said, his voice in her ear. "You know I never meant him to get hurt. I just wanted to. . ."

"Quiet. The police car's moving. It's coming in. It's moving towards us."

Ali moved her head slightly and saw around Stephen's shoulder. The sidelights of the police car were pointing at them about fifty metres away. The car was moving slowly, inching in their direction.

"What's it doing? Has it seen something?" Stephen said.

"It's too far away. It's too dark."

"Has it seen my car?"

It was coming closer. Ali held her breath. In her head, she wondered why she was hiding from them. Why not go out, run towards them, call them over, tell them what happened. *It was an accident.*

"It's stopped," Stephen said.

Ali looked past Stephen's shoulder as the passenger door opened. The inside of the car lit up for a moment as one of the officers got out. She couldn't see his face, but she did see the flash of a lighter and the tiny flame, there for a second and then gone.

"He's having a cigarette."

The driver's door opened and the other officer got out. They began to talk to each other across the bonnet of the car. Ali could hear their voices, but she couldn't make out what they were saying.

"How long are they going to be here?" Jackson said.

"I don't know."

"What are we going to do?"

"If you'd just let me think!"

They stood silently. Ali watched the two officers in the distance. Their voices rose and it sounded as though they were laughing at something. Beyond them, on the dual carriageway, something big must have gone past, because Ali could hear the lumbering of an engine, and she could feel vibrations underneath her feet, as though some distant earthquake was threatening.

"We'll have to hide his body."

"Why? What difference does it make?"

"If someone sees him in the morning, then there's a chance they'll find out that we're involved."

"I'm not involved!" Ali said.

"Ssh... Listen," Jackson said.

There was a high-pitched squeaking voice. The police-car radio. One policeman leaned into the driver's side and spoke on the radio. The other policeman was still smoking. Ali could just make out the pinprick of light from the cigarette. A voice came from inside the car. The engine started up. The policeman outside threw his cigarette into the air and got back into the car. The driver came forward and did a U-turn. At that moment someone must have turned the blue light on because it lit up the car park for a second, giving the place a blue-black hue. Then the car gathered speed, bumping over potholes and going around Harry's Diner. In a second it was gone.

The three of them walked out from behind the container.

"What are we going to do?"

"I don't know," Stephen said, his voice cracking, his hand clamping his forehead. "I don't know."

Jackson walked across to where Daniel was. He looked down at him. He had his back to them, but Ali could see his shoulders shaking. She knew he was crying.

The car park didn't seem as dark as it had before. All of a sudden she felt exposed, as though everyone could see her and Jackson and Stephen. As though everyone could *see* what they'd done. She went over to Daniel. She sat down on the tarmac beside him and she picked up his hand and held it.

NINETEEN

They were sitting in the car and the rain was spearing down.

Jackson and Stephen were in the front. Ali was in the back. Stephen and Jackson were talking, but she felt divorced from their words. As if this were some film she was watching, something that was happening to other people.

She looked at the clock on the dashboard. The time read 11.51. It had been just after eleven that they'd pulled off the A13 into Harry's Diner. Had it really only been forty minutes ago? It seemed like hours, as if they'd been there for ever, floundering about, arguing and fighting amid the weeds and the broken-down cars and the old container.

"We're going to have to leave him," Stephen said.

He turned round to her, staring at her, expecting a response.

"We could make an anonymous call," Jackson said.

"They find him tonight or in the morning and they might be able to work out who did this."

"It was an accident. None of us meant this to happen."

That was true. No one expected this. Ali knew that Jackson, so puffed up with indignation, so keen to get *respect*, did not consider anything like this. A few harsh words: pointing, threatening, posturing; these were the things that Jackson did. Stephen was the more experienced one. Stephen had been wild and run with bad boys. One day someone had walked up to him with a kitchen knife and slashed his face. Stephen had turned his life around with the help of his old teacher. All he had left was a jagged line down his cheek. *He* hadn't touched Daniel. He had tried to arbitrate, tried to make Jackson and Daniel *talk about it*. He'd tried to save face for Daniel, not allowing the ruckus to happen at his dad's wedding.

And now Daniel was dead.

Even though none of them meant it to happen.

"We need to hide his body and get away from here," Stephen said.

"I don't know."

"I've been in trouble with the police before. I know how this will look. The three of us conspired to get Daniel down here. Me and Ali picked him up off the street. We brought him here knowing you were going to have it out with him. We beat him up and he died."

"I never touched him," Ali said. "You never touched him!"

"I never actually *hit* him; I just didn't want him to get in the car!" Jackson said.

"But to outsiders it won't look like that. He took your girlfriend away. It'll look like revenge. You'll go to prison. Manslaughter. I'll go to prison. Conspiracy. I've got a record of violence. It'll look like I was a ringleader."

And what would happen to Ali? Would she end up in court, charged with a crime that she had no sense of being a part of? She got Daniel into the car. She lied to him about going to Hannah's. She was here, in the waste ground, when it all kicked off. Why hadn't she done something to stop it? She had a phone.

139

She could have rung for an ambulance. She could *still* ring for an ambulance.

But what was the point?

"If we hide his body, then no one will know what happened. It'll be days – or weeks, even – before he's found," Stephen said.

"Hide it? Where?"

They all looked out of the car window at the old container. Its door was hanging open, had been open for months. Stephen had thought, when they first parked up there, that some homeless person had been living in it, but it had been empty for a long time.

"In there?" Jackson said.

"We have to make a decision. We can't just hang around here. We've already had one police car passing through. We don't know who might have seen us. The longer we're here, the more likely it is that we'll get caught," Stephen said.

"There must be something else we can do," Ali said.

"There isn't. We can't do anything for him now. We have to look after ourselves."

What did he mean? Look after himself? All of them?

They certainly couldn't look after Daniel any more.

Stephen put his hands underneath Daniel Feeny's shoulders. He seemed to get a grip on Daniel's jacket. Jackson hooked his arms under Daniel's knees. Stephen made a count, *one, two, three,* and they both hoisted Daniel's inert body off the ground.

Ali looked away. The rain hit her face. She wiped it off with her hand and felt her hair damp around her ears.

This was not right. She knew it wasn't right, and yet she didn't have the will to stop it. All evening she'd been dragged along. Persuaded to go with Stephen and Jackson; pressured into getting Daniel in the car. It was as if she'd fallen in a river and tossed and turned and pulled towards a weir. Was that true, though? No one had forced her. Hadn't she been there because she wanted to spend time with Jackson? Doing anything? At any cost?

"Ali, help us! Hold the door wide open."

They were standing by the container. She reluctantly went across. She pulled the metal door open and felt a rush of stale air. Blackness seemed to balloon out of it.

"You can't put him in *there*," she said.

There was a dripping sound from inside. Water dripping from a hole somewhere. Ali got her mobile out and pressed the call button and the phone lit up the area for a second. It went black again and she pressed again, two, three times, so that the glow stayed on, a thin net of light, a luminous beam fighting a losing battle against the thick black interior.

"Come out of the way," Stephen said from behind.

There was a clattering sound as something dropped from somewhere.

"Quick, just get him in!" Stephen said, forcing past her, backing into the darkness.

She stepped away and saw, on the ground, a mobile. It had skittered away and she went across to pick it up. When she turned round, Stephen and Jackson were coming out of the container. Stephen closed the door and shot a bolt across at the top.

He walked towards her, taking his mobile out, looking intently at it. Jackson was still by the container. He was leaning forward, and a second later he dropped to his knees and began to be sick.

Ali looked down at the mobile in her hand.

"Is that Daniel's?" Stephen said.

"I think so."

"Get into the car. Take it with us. Throw it out while we're driving."

Stephen was businesslike. Behind her Jackson was sitting on the tarmac, his head in his hands.

"Let's get going!" Stephen said. "Let's get home."

They got into the car and drove away. After they'd gone a couple of miles, Ali wound the window down.

"Wait," Stephen said. "Wipe it over. You don't want any prints on it."

Ali wiped the mobile against her top and then tossed it out of the window. She wound the window up and leaned against the glass, watching the raindrops skidding along the surface, clinging to the car. She closed her eyes and listened as the wheels splashed through the surface water and the car sped on.

They stopped at the top of Jackson's street.

"Not a word to anyone," Stephen said.

"I know."

Jackson threw the car door open and got out. Ali watched him walk towards his house. He never said a word. He never turned round. He just got further and further away, and then he was gone.

Stephen drove off. He stopped the car outside his own house.

"You mustn't say a word to Hannah. Not a word," he said.

Ali didn't reply. She got out of the car and half walked, half ran home. Her mum and dad's car wasn't there, so she knew that they were still out at their friends'. When she got into her house, the lights were out. She stood in the hallway with her back against the front door. Her eyes got used to the dark and she could make out the stairs and the hall table and doors of the rooms on the ground floor.

Not like the container.

That had been the blackest dark she'd ever seen. Like a coffin.

TWENTY
Year Thirteen

At three-thirty the college was emptying out. Alison got a drink from one of the machines and took it outside. She sat on a bench, looking round in case Jackson should appear.

It was warm even though the sky had clouded over. She had on a short-sleeved T-shirt and cut-off trousers. On her feet she wore sandals. Her toenails were painted a pearly pink. She'd done them that morning after having a shower. She didn't know why. Nail varnish and make-up were things she didn't really bother with, and yet when she was drying herself, she saw the bottle of nail varnish sitting on the shelf amid her mum's things. It was the tiniest bottle and had a silver lid and looked jewel-like, as if it wouldn't be out of place hanging on a pendant. She unscrewed the lid and the brush came out coated in pearlized paint. It had only taken a few moments to cover her toenails and she'd sat for a while afterwards allowing them to dry, looking at her feet from different angles, holding them up under the light to get a better idea of the colour. It was a short chunk of time when she'd given herself something

144

mindless to do, something that gave her a little bit of pleasure.

Now they didn't look so good. They were just rhinestones, a bit of fake glitter. It gave her a dragging ache in her chest that she should enjoy something so slight, so small, so superficial when there was this huge unspeakable thing in her life. She stood up from the bench and she could almost feel the long grey shadow that hung on the ground behind her, weighing her down, holding her back.

Where was Jackson? A beep came from her mobile.

Change of plans. Meet me at Blackwood by the old changing rooms.

She should have been upset, but really it didn't matter. She had nowhere she had to be. She pulled together the straps of her bag and hoisted them over her shoulder, then headed out of college in the direction of the park.

Blackwood Park was bathed in sunshine. Some of the boats were out on the lake. She bypassed them and started on the path up to the sports centre and the games courts. Her bag was heavy on her shoulder and she felt hot and immediately thirsty even though she'd just had a drink at college.

She paused for a moment to get her breath.

Jackson was going to give himself up to the police.

It was hard to believe, and yet wasn't there a bit of her that hadn't been surprised? Of the three of them, he had been the one to fall apart. Stephen had distanced himself.

She had thrown herself into as many activities as she could. But Jackson had been brittle. Just a hug might have broken his bones, so she'd stood back away from him.

She was nearing the sports centre. She could hear a cheer from the football courts beyond, a game in progress.

Jackson had worn his grief on his face. He had been inconsolable. It had been his fault. It had all started with him. He had disliked Daniel, and maybe on some deep level he had wanted it to happen. Stephen had told him to pull himself together. Stephen had been afraid that Jackson would open up and let it all pour out. In those days after Daniel's body was found, Alison had tried to look after him, but one day he slipped out of her fingers and the next thing she heard was that he'd gone to Brighton to live permanently with his brother.

She walked past the tennis courts and saw the wall of trees along the edge. The leaves and branches swayed gently in the breeze, but underneath it looked like night. When she stepped out of the sun, she felt the chill of the shade. In the back of her head she heard "Fifteen love! Deuce! Thirty love!" from the courts and the bounce of a ball and the thwack of a return serve.

She went through the trees. He was there. Sitting at one of the picnic tables. She sat down opposite him, placing her heavy bag on the table.

"Have you been to the police yet?" she said, her voice hushed.

He shook his head.

"Have you changed your mind?"

He shook his head again. She sat up and looked at him.

"You know that Stephen's right? If the truth comes out, he will come off worse than you or me."

Even as she said this, she knew it wasn't the whole picture. She was talking about Stephen and Jackson's truth. If the *whole* truth came out, it would be she who got the worst punishment – *she* who people would look at with disgust.

"I can't help that. I'm just doing what I should have done two years ago."

"Have you thought about your mum?"

He nodded. A ghost of something passed across his face: shame, fear, maybe both together.

"And Hannah?"

Neither of them spoke. What would Hannah say? How would she feel when she knew that it was the three of them who had killed Daniel and that it all happened in her name? Alison pictured Hannah in her mum's hairdresser's. Maybe she'd be cutting someone's hair, fluffing it up with a comb, holding a round mirror to the back of the customer's head. On the ground, under the mirror, would be Hannah's stripy bag or a newer version of it. Hannah, who never left her house without hair tongs, make-up, gel, moisturizer, magazine, spare shoes, tissues and anything else she thought she might need. Hannah, who seemed superficial but wasn't. She had given up Jackson for someone odd like Daniel. She had been *touched* by Daniel's suicide attempt. Alison remembered the day that Hannah had been straight with her. It was the last time they'd spoken before that night. *You might be going to Cambridge and I might be working in a hairdresser's, but I'm not stupid.*

What would Hannah think when she found out?

"I came here to look at the place again," Jackson said. "To look at the tree."

"You have to push it out of your mind."

"But doesn't it creep up on you? You know, when you're shopping or buying a Big Mac, don't you stop and think about Daniel locked in that container? Doesn't that, like, *colour* everything else you do?"

Alison didn't answer. She did shop and she sometimes had a McDonald's. She went to college, she worked in the charity shop, she made sure every moment of her day was full up, crammed end to end with things to do. That way she could hold it at bay. At night-time it was a different matter.

"Do you remember that night we saved his life?"

She nodded.

"I think about that a lot. About him sitting on this tree, about the moment he dropped from the branch. If we'd only left him. It would have only taken him minutes to die, seconds even. Like turning a light off."

She knew what Jackson was thinking. How preferable it would have been for Daniel to die that night instead of later in a car park off the A13.

"I think about it all the time," he said miserably.

"It won't do anyone any good to drag it all up again," she said softly.

He didn't answer. He didn't say a word.

If they could just hold their nerve. If they could just see this through, pull Jackson back from the edge of this cliff where he was standing. Make him see that he could bear it all, the way she and Stephen had managed to do. She lifted her hand and put it over Jackson's.

"I've missed you," she said.

He nodded. Had he missed her?

"I can't think of anything but Daniel at this moment," he said. "After I've been to the police, after it's all out in the open, after I've had my punishment – then I'll be able to think of other things," he said, lifting his hand slightly so that her fingers laced in with his.

"I know," she said.

But Jackson didn't go to the police the next day.

Or the one after that. He didn't have to.

Stephen Grainger got there first.

TWENTY-ONE

Year Eleven

On the day after they killed Daniel Feeny, Ali expected the police to knock on her door. A heavy hand thumping at the wood. A line of officers standing on her pathway.

The whole of Sunday she waited for it. She tried to do normal things: sorting out her stuff now that the exams had finished, looking through her wardrobe for things she wanted to get rid of, tidying up her room. She offered to help cook dinner, but her mum shooed her away, asking her to go with her dad and pick up Gran in time for Sunday lunch.

She checked her mobile from time to time. She was dreading seeing the message icon in case it was bad news, and yet every time she looked and saw the screen staring back blankly at her, she felt a sting of disappointment. Neither Stephen nor Jackson had contacted her. She didn't care about Stephen, but she had hoped that Jackson might send a message. She thought of contacting him, but somehow she couldn't. She didn't know what to say. Everything seemed too trivial, and the really big thing, the thing she wanted to talk about, was too awful to put into tiny words on the screen of a mobile.

At about one o'clock, she got into her dad's hot car and they drove the short distance to pick up her gran. It started to rain, lightly at first, then heavier, the drops pinging on the roof of the car.

"You all right today?" her dad said.

"Yes."

"You seem a bit quiet. Still upset about breaking up with your boyfriend?"

She didn't answer.

Once she was in her gran's, Ali went round the house, closing some of the windows so that the rain didn't get in. Her gran was fiddling round, putting a cardigan on. Then she spent a few moments looking for her handbag, a black leather pouch that usually hung from her shoulder by a thin strap.

"My keys?" her gran said.

"They're in your bag, Gran. You just put them there."

They had their lunch just after two. Her gran's dog, Rex, ran around the table looking for titbits, and her mum instructed her and her dad not to feed him. Her gran took no notice. She slipped a bit of meat down to the dog and then gave a little laugh, as if sharing a joke with Rex.

After lunch, Ali offered to wash up. The others sat in the living room watching a film. As the rain pattered against the window, Ali started the long job of clearing up after the Sunday roast. She was glad of the activity. She took her time, rearranging bits of the cupboard when she replaced dishes and cutlery. When there was absolutely nothing left to do, she picked up her mobile and looked at the screen.

No one had called.

She thought about Daniel's dad and his new wife. She wondered what was going on at their house. She felt a dragging sensation in her gut. For the first time she thought about going to the police station herself. Walking in and telling them what had happened. If she described how it just all got out of hand, wouldn't people understand?

The doorbell sounded. It startled her because she'd stopped expecting to hear it. She went out to the hall and opened the front door. Stephen was standing at the end of her pathway. He had his sunglasses hooked in the front of his shirt.

"Has something happened?" she said, walking up to him.

He shook his head. He was looking down the street, not making eye contact. "You?"

"No."

"We need to meet. The three of us. There's things that need to be sorted out. Four o'clock at the lake in Blackwood. That way it looks like we're just out for the afternoon."

She nodded.

Stephen's mouth was in a crooked line. He was touching it with the tips of his fingers.

"I already told Jackson."

He walked off without another word. As Ali went back into the house, she saw her dad was smirking.

"I knew that lad wouldn't give up!" he said, winking at her.

At ten to four she left the house. The rain had stopped and it seemed warm. She wondered what Stephen wanted to say. Perhaps he was thinking about going to the police. He had given no sign, but why not? After a night to think about it, surely it was the most sensible thing to do. But would Jackson want that? Last night he had acted stupidly, childishly. His ridiculous pride had got them into this. And he'd been the one who was physical with Daniel, pulling him out of the car. It was his fault, but she couldn't blame just him. Hadn't she been the one who let him know about Daniel and Hannah? She'd told him deliberately. Just so that she could catch his attention.

Now someone was dead. Two things: a conversation on the mobile and a dead boy; how could these be linked?

When she got to the park, she saw that Stephen was standing by the place that hired boats out. Jackson was a few metres away. They were speaking to each other. She hurried on.

"This won't take long," Stephen said, when she got up to them.

The three of them stood awkwardly in a loose triangle.

"We were all a bit emotional last night. I think I'd better be clear about what we decided."

Ali looked down at the grass. *She* hadn't decided anything.

"What happened was the worst thing. None of us meant..." He stopped and looked around, waiting for some nearby people to pass. His voice dropped lower. "I don't know when the body will be found. But when it is, there'll be an investigation. I don't know if we'll even be part of it, but we have to be absolutely clear on what we were doing last night."

Jackson looked pale. His lips were cracked. She looked down at his wrist and saw that his leather band was still there. Hers was in her drawer. She didn't feel right wearing it now.

"Ali, are you listening?"

"Yes."

"So Jackson came round my place. We decided to go for a drive and I called for you. Even though we're not together, we're still friends. The three of us went out for a drive. Let's say we went up to the Queen Elizabeth Bridge and up to Hornchurch. We didn't stop. We got back about twelve-thirty. I drove Jackson home, then you. That's it. That's what we did. We don't change our story. Nothing."

There was silence, and the three of them stood awkwardly.

"We should go to the police," Ali said. "There's no way we can cover this up."

Stephen rolled his eyes.

"When they do find his body, it won't take them long to find out that Daniel took Jackson's girlfriend behind his back."

"But Hannah never told him about that. As of now, Jackson thinks that his girlfriend just got fed up."

"I rang him and told him."

"Only you and Jackson know about that."

"Are you going to go along with this?" Ali said to Jackson.

"I have to."

A family were passing by. They had just bought tickets and were hiring a rowing boat. Two young boys ran ahead. One picked one boat and the other picked a different one. The parents laughed.

"We could all go together to the police station," she said. "Explain it. Tell the truth."

Jackson looked straight at her. He frowned and for a second he seemed to sway. Then Stephen shook his head.

"It's too late to go. We have to stick with it. Just act like we normally would. You go to school or whatever. I go to work. We don't contact each other about it by mobile. We just carry on."

"It's easy for you to say that..."

"This is not easy for me, Ali. Whatever you think, this is by far the most horrible thing that has ever happened to me."

Stephen's eyes looked tiny, sunken.

Ali's throat was tight. She was not going to cry. She was not.

Jackson began to pick at his lips. Stephen started to speak again but stopped for a second. It looked as though he was getting upset. His neck had reddened.

"I wanted to help Dan. I liked him. I really liked the lad," he said, his voice breaking. "I wanted to help him make something of his life and instead of that..."

Jackson turned away, looking out of the park towards the road. Ali stared at Stephen. His eyes had glassed over. Around them people were walking this way and that. Some people were queuing up at the Italian ice cream place. A baby in a pushchair went by, holding a cone of white whipped ice cream that was already running over his hands. Ali put her finger out to touch Stephen's arm.

"Don't," he said.

He pulled a handkerchief out of his trouser pocket and turned away. He walked towards the lake. Ali watched him go.

"I've got to go," Jackson said.

She stood still as he walked off. She wanted to go after him but her feet wouldn't take her. She held her legs rigid in case they quivered and gave way.

She stood on her own in Blackwood for a long time.

The next day she tried to carry on as normal.

It was Monday, but school was finished and she had very little to do. Her mum and dad were out at work, so she did some housework. She worked feverishly. She vacuumed the living room, moving the furniture out of the way and back again. She dusted the picture rail, the skirting boards, the furniture, the door handles. She polished the mirrors and the glass panes in the front door. She unzipped the cushion covers and plumped up the cushions.

How long would it be until someone found Daniel?

Days? A week? A month?

She abandoned the vacuum cleaner and went up to her room and lay on the bed, her knees up to her chest. It was the beginning of the summer holidays. It was supposed to be a good time. The end of her time at school. No more exams. Over the next week she only had to go in and get a number of forms signed, return books and say goodbye to teachers. Then, on Friday, five days away, was the year eleven leavers' assembly. The last event of her secondary school career.

She had been looking forward to it. The previous year she had been one of the year ten students who had helped set it up. The students had been allowed to wear their own clothes and the assembly was a special one. The chairs were arranged in a horseshoe and there were bowls of flowers and soft music played.

The year eleven students came into school looking smart. They congregated in the garden area of the playground, a place that was only used on special occasions. They sat on benches or stood among the shrubs and trees, looking slightly awkward. Only weeks before, they'd been slouching round the playground or the corridors, moaning and groaning about teachers and work and the annoying younger kids. On the day of the last assembly, many of them broke into tears and looked longingly at the dusty school playground and the stuffy classrooms.

The assembly had had a churchlike feel to it, the year elevens shuffling along the rows, looking grown up and nervous at the same time. Ali had watched from the side as they had been given their goodbyes, the head of year eleven and the deputy standing up and waving them off as if they were hundreds of small boats taking off from a quay.

Now Ali would be at the assembly hearing that goodbye.

She closed her eyes and pushed her face into the pillow. The word *goodbye* was heavy and solid, like a door closing on the past. A door shut tight. A dark room beyond. A tiny space; a boy lying face down. She couldn't help but picture the container. Stephen had said that he thought people sometimes slept there in the winter, homeless people.

Now it wasn't a place to sleep; it was a place of death.

Her mobile sounded. She picked it off her bedside cabinet. On the screen she read *Hannah*.

Hannah who knew nothing.

She sat up on the bed. She considered letting the call go to voicemail but then decided to take it.

"Hi," she said lightly, her shoulders stiff with apprehension.

"Hi, Ali. Have you seen Dan?"

"No."

"Funny. No one's seen him. Or heard from him. Not since his dad's wedding."

"Oh," Ali said, licking her lips.

There was a moment's quiet. Ali tried to think of something normal to say.

"He had an argument with his dad and left the reception early," Hannah said.

Ali remembered Daniel walking along the road that led away from the Rainham Hotel. He'd been wearing a suit. A proper grown-up suit like the kind that Stephen wore for work.

"Have you asked Stephen? Maybe he's seen him."

"Yep! I'll do that. Odd, though. His dad's a bit worried, you know, with what happened up at Blackwood."

"Yes. I can understand that. He seemed pretty happy when I saw you with him last week."

"Yes, he is. Maybe he's lost his mobile. Oh well, I'll ring Stephen."

The call ended and Ali sat holding her mobile up to her chest. Lying had been easier than she'd thought.

TWENTY-TWO

Jackson came round in the evening. It gave her a start when she saw him on the doorstep. He looked tired. His hair was sticking up. He was wearing his cut-offs and trainers and an oversized black T-shirt that seemed to drain the colour out of him.

Her mum and dad were in the kitchen clearing up after dinner, so she took him into the living room.

"Hannah rang," she said.

"I know. She rang Stephen and he called me."

"She didn't ring you?"

He shook his head.

She felt relieved at this. It meant that Hannah didn't think Jackson had any knowledge of Daniel's whereabouts; she didn't even *consider* him as someone who might know where Daniel was.

A second later she felt full of remorse for even thinking like this.

"Stephen wants us to meet him on the high street. He's worried about something. He wouldn't say what. He didn't want to ring you," Jackson said, lowering his voice on the word *ring*.

"Why not? I thought he said phone calls were all right?"

"Yeah, but someone might ask why there's a sudden spate of calls between us three."

"Who might ask?"

"I don't know! The police? I don't know. Stephen's just being careful."

The police. The words made her feel weak.

"Why does he want us to meet?"

"I don't know. But we should make a move."

Ali got her money and her mobile and told her mum that she was going out.

"Are you seeing that lad?" her mum said. "I thought he was Hannah's boyfriend."

Ali just shook her head tersely.

"I was only saying," her mum called after her.

Stephen's car was parked down a side street. He grunted when they got in.

"Everything all right with Hannah's call?"

She nodded.

"What's up?" Jackson said.

"CCTV cameras."

"What about them?"

"Were there any? On Saturday night?"

"In that yard? It's just a dump. There was nothing valuable there."

"I know that, but the café is in the front and I'm just wondering whether there were cameras on it. On the parking bays. And if there were, whether those cameras might have picked us up driving through and into the back lot."

"I don't know. I never looked."

"I've got no idea," Ali said.

"We need to find out. I don't want to park there and get out and look. I'll drive past a couple of times and you two need to look carefully."

"What about cameras on the A13?" Jackson said.

"We have to check that as well. There aren't any speed cameras around there, I know that for sure..."

Stephen started up the car and they drove off. Ten minutes later they were on the A13. It was still light, the sun slipping down the horizon, leaving a burn mark on the sky. After a while they saw the Ford factory as big as a small town, throwing its massive shadow over the road. When they got closer, the neon sign of Harry's Diner could be seen on the opposite side. Stephen slowed down. A lorry behind him gave him an irritated hoot and then eased out and began to overtake him. Ali looked hard at the road coming up to the café. She couldn't see any cameras at all. When they came up parallel to the café, Jackson spoke.

"There's a camera. Right over the main entrance. It's pointing away from the café, towards the parking bays. It's just a small one. I don't think its angle would include the entrance off the dual carriageway."

But Ali wasn't really listening. She was moving her head to see if she could see behind the café to the old container. It wasn't possible, but in her head she imagined she'd seen it: brown, solid, bolted up, impenetrable.

They were past it by the time Jackson had finished speaking. Ali turned round and looked out the back window of the car as it got further away. She hadn't noticed the camera at all.

"It might move, though. Some cameras rotate. We need to check that. We'll look again," Stephen said, heading off the dual carriageway, on to a roundabout. "This time check for cameras on the road."

"I did. I already did," Ali said.

"Check again."

They drove up the other side of the dual carriageway. Stephen slowed again as they passed the café. Ali's eyes searched each side of the road for traffic cameras.

"The camera outside the café hasn't moved," Jackson said.

"Are you sure?"

"I'm sure."

They had passed the café again and were heading back towards home. A mile or so on, Ali saw a row of traffic cameras attached to a metal cradle over the road.

"Those are the closest cameras," Ali said.

"That's good."

Stephen drove on, gathering speed until the slip road off the A13. The radio was on playing songs that Ali usually liked. Tonight they made her feel anxious and unhappy. The cheeriness of the tune, the vitality of the singer, the pleasure of the beat; these things made her ache. She realized then that not one of them had said a word about Daniel and the fact that he was dead. It was as if it had been forgotten. Now they were just making sure that they wouldn't get caught.

Stephen slowed down as they left the dual carriageway and moved on to local roads, heading for home. It was almost dark. The rear lights of cars in front looked like red eyes.

"I think we're all right. I don't think any of those cameras will pick anything up."

Ali didn't answer him. What was the point? She wasn't *all*

right. She looked out of the window at the shops and houses flashing past. She felt her eyes blurring and blinked back the tears.

Stephen pulled the car up in a street near the park.

"When do you think they'll find him?" Jackson said.

"I don't know."

"Maybe they'll never find him," Ali said.

"Maybe. That's why we've got to stay calm. Keep to our story. We didn't mean it to happen, but it did. There's no reason why we should go to prison for something that we never meant."

"I still think. . ." Ali started.

"You know what, Ali, I'm sick to death of you whining on." Stephen's voice was sharp.

"Leave it out, mate. Don't get on at Ali. If you want to have a go at someone, have a go at me," Jackson said.

"You're right. I'm just upset."

Stephen pulled up. They were on the high street, across from the tube station.

"Sorry, Ali."

Ali gave a stiff nod and threw the door of the car open and got out. Jackson got out of the passenger side. The car drove off and they were left together on the street. Opposite them, hanging around outside the station, were some kids from school. They called over to Jackson and he waved back. Then they started frolicking about, playing some sort of silly game. A couple of them had bottles of beer and one of the girls, who Ali had been friendly with in previous years, offered them some. Ali shook her head and walked on. Jackson spoke to some of the boys, then caught her up.

"I don't want you to think I'm all right with all this. I'm not."

"I know," she said.

"I just didn't know what to do," he said, holding his hands out helplessly.

"I know."

"I wish we'd rung an ambulance or gone to the police. I wish we'd carried him into the car, taken him to the hospital. Anything. I wish we'd done anything rather than just leave him there."

"We could now," Ali said, stopping, grabbing his arm. "We could."

"But it wouldn't change anything, and Stephen would go to prison as well as me. He has a record of violence. No one would believe that he hadn't been involved."

She walked on. *I don't care about Stephen*, she wanted to say.

"It's like this is the road we've chosen and we've got to see it through. You know, if I thought for one second that going to the police would change a single thing, I'd do it."

She couldn't think of anything to say.

"I'm going back down to Brighton next week. I'm going to stay there until college in the autumn. I think it's for the best."

He was running away. She linked her arm through his, her fingers on his skin.

"Don't go," she said.

He stopped and put his arm round her and pulled her close.

"I have to. Otherwise I'll go mad."

164

TWENTY-THREE

Ali stood by the window in Mrs Caine's room.

She was waiting for the teacher to return so that she could have a final tutorial before officially leaving school. She was wearing her school uniform for the last time. She wriggled around in it, feeling as though it wasn't fitting right. The skirt felt too tight and the blouse looked grey instead of white. Mrs Caine had told her to have a seat in her room, but she'd felt too restless to sit down. The beeps went for the end of the morning session. Soon it would be lunch time. Not that she felt hungry.

She hadn't slept well. She'd gone to bed too early and woken up at about two and tossed and turned for what seemed like hours. She finally got back to sleep but woke up at 6.17, the sun glowing round the edges of her bedroom curtains. She would have got up then, but the only thing she had to do that day was to see Mrs Caine and return some books to the school library. The rest of the day was like an empty sheet of paper. So she lay in bed. The radio was on and it blocked out her thoughts. From time to time she heard the sounds of her mum and dad getting ready for work. After hearing the front door bang for the second time when her mum left for the surgery, she turned over and pulled the sheet up over her head.

She lay in the darkness and thought about Daniel.

It had been two and a half days since they'd left him.

Sixty hours. She groaned and her stomach gnawed at her. She hadn't eaten much over the last couple of days. Cups of coffee and half-eaten bits of toast. Most of the time she felt light-headed.

Now the door opened and Mrs Caine came in.

"Sorry, Alison. I had to see a couple of students. Now, take a seat."

Mrs Caine looked cool and crisp. Her nails were the same shade of pink as her blouse and her glasses had slipped down her nose. She pushed them up with a single finger.

"Your last exam was a week ago. Now you have the summer break and A-levels at East London College to look forward to. That's a very good college. Their arts faculty is excellent. I imagine your A-levels will go very well there. Remember, though: you can't afford to sit back. You have to work hard from the first day. Four A-levels is a tough load, but I know you can do it and I don't want you to lose sight of Cambridge."

Mrs Caine looked up at her.

Ali nodded. Cambridge, Dagenham; Dagenham, Cambridge. What did it matter where she went?

"That's not the only thing I wanted to talk to you about. I expect you know that Daniel Feeny has gone missing. It's extremely worrying after what happened some weeks back." Mrs Caine coughed lightly. "After the attempted. . ."

Ali's lips were fused together. There was no need to say the word *suicide*.

"Mr Feeny is concerned that his son might try it again. I understand your boyfriend was quite friendly with him?"

"Yes, but he hasn't seen him since before his dad's wedding."

"I believe Mr Feeny has been to the police. I understand that they may wish to speak to you and your boyfriend. And others who had spent time with Daniel."

Ali nodded. "Stephen's not my boyfriend any more. We split up."

"Ah," Mrs Caine said.

The police wanted to speak to them.

"The police are looking for Daniel but, you know, if someone wants to stay away..." She shrugged.

Mrs Caine meant that Daniel *might never be found.*

Ali was suddenly full of emotion. She needed to blow her nose. She felt in her pocket and pulled out a tissue.

"Oh, Alison, don't cry."

She couldn't help it. The tears came quickly, great splashes on her cheek; her tissue was soaked in seconds.

"Don't get yourself upset, Alison. I'm sure Daniel will turn up."

She nodded.

"I'll see you at the leavers' assembly on Friday. Maybe we'll have some good news by then."

After going to the girls' toilets and grabbing a wad of tissue, she passed by the lunch hall. She saw Hannah sitting in the middle of a group of girls. She stepped back, to the edge of the door, and looked in. Hannah was upset. One of the girls had an arm around her shoulder. She couldn't hear what was being said, but the voices were weighed down with sympathy. What did Hannah think? That Daniel had tried to kill himself again? That he would

167

be found in some part of the forest? Curled up somewhere with a bottle of tablets next to him? Hannah was crying for what she thought might have happened to her boyfriend. Ali was crying because she *knew*.

She walked off. It was hot. Her clothes were tight and she pulled at the waistband of her skirt and put her finger inside the collar of her blouse. Up ahead, the corridor seemed to get narrower. There was just no air. The strip lights glared an ugly yellow that hurt her eyes.

The police wanted to speak to them.

She burst out of the doors and into the playground. The brightness hit her. The tarmac of the playground felt soft beneath her shoes, like treacle. She made her way through groups of students until she got to the far end of the play area and headed for the lane that led to the front gate of the school. She walked along it, looking down at the shadow that had fallen in front of her. An indistinct shape of darkness that mirrored her.

She got to the end of the lane and turned out of the school. She walked along the main road until she reached her bus stop and then stood there waiting. Her bus was seven minutes away. The display board showed it as the third one due to arrive. She sat on one of the seats and she thought of Daniel sitting next to Hannah in the bus shelter that day when she first saw them together.

She welled up, tears blurring her vision. She was crying again.

All she had wanted was for Jackson to notice her. That was why she'd told him. A phone call. How had it moved from being a phone call to. . .? She couldn't say the word. It hovered at the edge of her mind. A dark shape like a bird in the sky.

Murder.

She couldn't live with this. She *wouldn't* live with it.

When the bus came, she got on it. She got out her mobile and sent the same text to Jackson and Stephen.

It was gone eight and they were sitting in Stephen's car on the edge of Blackwood Park. They'd been stationary for some minutes. Ali was in the back and Jackson was in the front. Stephen was staring straight ahead. His left hand was holding on to the steering wheel, his middle finger tapping lightly.

"Mrs Caine said that the police will want to speak to us," Ali said.

"That's routine," Stephen said.

"I'm going to tell them what happened."

Neither of them answered her, and as they sat there, the silence seemed to stack up like a brick wall between them.

"I can't keep this horrible thing inside me."

Ali looked out of the window. They were adjacent to the lake at Blackwood Park. It was still light and she could see a couple of dogs tearing across the grass, following a Frisbee that looked as if it were floating in the air.

"We agreed we would not say anything," Stephen said.

Jackson wound down the window.

"How can we carry on as if nothing's happened?" Ali protested.

Even though the window was open, the air was heavy. Ali was sitting forward, agitated. She put her hand out and touched Jackson's shoulder.

"We have to tell someone," she whispered as if it were only the two of them in the car.

He didn't answer.

Some boys were on their bikes. They were riding slowly, their front wheels turning from side to side to keep their balance. They were laughing, joking with each other, having a good time.

"We can't," Stephen said. "Not now. It's too late."

"What about Daniel's dad? Doesn't he have a right to know where his son is?" Ali said.

"You think that's going to make him feel any better?"

"It might be better if he thought that Daniel had run away," Jackson said.

"If a police officer interviews me, then I'm going to tell the truth."

"Then me and Jackson will go to prison."

Why was Stephen doing all the talking?

"Jackson, we should go. It's the right thing to do. It was an accident."

Jackson shook his head but didn't speak.

"I'm not going to sit here any more," Ali said, feeling for the door handle. "I've told you what I'm going to do."

Ali let the door swing open and got out of the car. She stood in the road and felt the cool air hit her. She was momentarily disoriented. She turned in the direction of home and started to walk but stopped moments later and went into the park. She walked along, puffed up, sidestepping boys playing with a football and two dogs having a play fight. She walked on, her chin trembling, her ears feeling like they were on fire.

She glanced back at the car. The two of them were still sitting there.

How could they be so cold?

She would tell the police everything.

TWENTY-FOUR

The police came to see her on Wednesday morning.

Her mum and dad had gone to work, so the house was empty. She was sitting watching daytime television when the bell sounded. She opened her front door and a young WPC was standing there.

"Alison Rose?" she said brightly.

Ali nodded.

"WPC Emma Myers. I'm here to talk to you about Daniel Feeny?"

"Come in," Ali said, her voice steady.

She led the way down the hallway to the kitchen. The WPC chatted about the weather.

"It's too hot! People like the sunshine, but for someone like me who's walking round all day, it's a killer! I'm sure I lose a couple of pounds every day. Oh! That's a laugh. If I lost that much weight I'd be like Kate Moss!"

"Can I get you a cold drink?"

"Some water would be good," the WPC said. "This stuff is so heavy."

Ali looked. She was pointing at her belt, which held a radio and truncheon and notebook. Her trousers looked like they were made from heavy-drill cotton and her shoes were black lace-ups.

The WPC took her hat off. Ali was surprised to see that her hair had been dyed a white blonde. It was short and had been flattened on top by the hat, so the officer ran her fingers through it. The thing that struck Ali was how *young* she looked. Without her hat, sitting at her kitchen table, she didn't look much older than she or Hannah did.

She opened the fridge door and got some water out and poured it into a glass. She took her time doing it and kept her back to the officer for longer than necessary. She was ready for this. She had worked out what she was going to say, how she was going to word it. When she turned round, the officer was staring straight at her. On the table, opened up, was a notebook.

I have to tell you something about Daniel, she was going to start.

"Can I just say," the WPC said, "how much I admired what you and your friends did for Daniel."

Ali made a dismissive gesture with her hand, but the officer continued talking.

"I'll let you into a secret. I'd only just started the job that week. Finished my training a week or so before, so I was brand new. I was sitting round the station shadowing other officers, so I had a bit of time on my hands, and I read all the reports of the attempted suicide. You and your friends were really brave. Most kids would have run a mile from that. They'd have left it for someone else to clear up. Have you ever thought of becoming a police officer?"

Ali was thrown by the question. She was getting ready to play down her role that night at Blackwood. It was on the tip of her tongue to praise Stephen and Jackson. To let the young woman see who had really been courageous. But the question at the end had put her off track.

"No," she said, "I've never thought of being a police officer."

But even as she said it, a memory came back to her from years before, when she was a little girl. When her gran had picked her up from school and looked after her until her mum came home from work. She saw a momentary image of an ambulance parked by the side of the road. There'd been a policewoman there, kneeling over a motorcyclist who'd been knocked off his bike. Her gran had stood and watched for a minute but then seemed to realize that she had Ali's hand in hers. She made clucking noises and pulled her out of the way. But not before Ali had seen the WPC push people back, away from the man. Then she'd talked into a radio that had been fixed to her shoulder. Her voice was loud and clear and in seconds Ali heard a siren and had thought, then, at that young age, that the ambulance had appeared because the policewoman had summoned it. For a long time after that, Ali played games where she was the police officer and her dolls were accident victims.

"That's a shame," the WPC said. "It's a really good career. Most young women are put off by the uniform. I know that's a sexist thing to say, but..."

Ali gave a weak smile, not quite sure how to respond to these friendly overtones.

"So, getting back to business. You've seen Daniel a couple of times since that night when he tried to commit suicide? How has he seemed to you?"

Ali sat down on the chair facing the officer. She braced herself, ready to tell her story.

I saw him on Saturday night and there was a row and things got out of hand and Daniel got into a tussle with Jackson...

A ringtone sounded. The WPC put her finger up in the air.

"That's me," she said. "It's a work call. Do you mind if I take it in the hallway? I'll just be a minute."

Ali shrugged. When the officer stood up, Ali could have sworn she smelled a rush of scent. She stretched her arms out and felt her bones cracking. While she waited, another thing about the accident came back to her. It was the day after, she thought, or a few days after, and she'd heard her gran telling her mum that the boy on the motorcycle had been killed. She'd been in the corner of the room and her ears pricked up, because at that very moment she'd been playing a robbery where a couple of her soft toys had been sticking up a bank and her policewoman doll had stopped them outside. Her policewoman doll had been holding a gun then, and she'd made them all lie face down on the ground and her soft toys had been arrested. When her gran mentioned the motorcyclist, she'd listened. Her gran said that he'd cried for his mum and then died. She'd scooped up her soft toys and flung them in the corner and sat with the policewoman on her lap and imagined the boy crying for his mum. It had given her a terrible feeling of anguish, as if it had been *her* on the ground crying for her mum.

The kitchen door opened.

"Sorry about that! I'm due to visit a secondary school later today – not yours – and that was the teacher rearranging the time. Now, where were we?"

"You were asking me how I thought Daniel was," Ali said.

"Yes, did he seem depressed? Did he give you any indication that he was upset?"

Daniel had an argument with Jackson over Hannah...

"I only saw him a couple of times since. He seemed OK. It was Hannah and Stephen who saw him most."

"That's right. I've seen Hannah. I'm seeing Stephen this evening."

"The thing is..."

Daniel had an accident in this deserted car park in Dagenham...

"Did Daniel mention any other friends that he might have gone to stay with? Did he say anything about his father getting remarried?"

She shook her head. She hadn't expected to be asked this kind of stuff. She needed to start talking about what happened. She wanted more than anything to get the words out, to tell this woman, this girl, what had happened.

"Look, Daniel and Hannah got together..."

"Yes, Hannah said. What about her previous boyfriend? Ryan Jackson? Wasn't he upset?"

"I'm not sure..."

"Hannah seems like a really nice girl..."

She nodded politely. If the WPC would stop just for a moment, if she would give her time and space, she might be able to say what she wanted to say. She put her hand up to her neck and rubbed it. Her skin was hot, fiery.

"And Ryan Jackson wasn't involved?"

Ali faltered. "What do you mean?"

"Of the four of you, he didn't have anything to do with Daniel at all? After that night at Blackwood? Have I got that right?"

"Yes, he didn't want to get involved."

The WPC started to write on her pad, her head down. Now she would say her piece, now she would explain.

Daniel thought Jackson was OK about him going out with Hannah. But Jackson was angry. His pride had been hurt, and then Stephen got involved. He wanted to try to sort it so that they didn't come to blows at Daniel's dad's wedding.

"So when was it that you last saw Daniel?"

Ali stared at the WPC. Her face was so sincere. Her skin looked white and seemed to merge in with her hair. She was pretty and nice and Ali suddenly couldn't face telling her. She looked down at the wooden table. The grain was all going one way, but just in front of her was a knot in the wood. It was like an eye looking up at her. She focused on it until it blurred.

"Don't get upset!" the WPC said.

There were tears coming down her face. She hardly noticed them. She'd become immune to crying.

"I'm sure he'll turn up. Teenage boys often go off. It's a rite of passage thing. The only reason we're following it up so closely is because of his recent suicide attempt. If he is depressed or upset, then he might do something, and we don't want that to happen."

The WPC stood up. "Look, you know who I am. Emma Myers. If you want to talk about Daniel or if you can think of anything else that might help, then give me a ring at the station. I might not be there to speak to, but if you leave a message, I'll get back to you."

176

Ali wiped her face with the ends of her fingers and then she offered the WPC a small bottle of water to take out with her, but she turned it down.

"Ring me if Daniel should contact you," the WPC said, walking off down the path, out into the bright sunshine.

After closing the front door, Ali went back up the hallway. She went into the living room and turned the television on again.

She hadn't been able to tell it.

Maybe it didn't matter any more. Maybe no one would ever find the body and Daniel's dad would just think that his son had run away.

But someone did find his body.

She heard about it two days later at the leavers' assembly.

TWENTY-FIVE

Year Thirteen

Her room was haunted. She had known this for two years.

Each time it started, the fear crept up, slid its hand round her throat, enveloped her, smothered her.

As if it were the first time all over again.

Now that the noises had stopped, the room seemed to settle under a thick coat of black. Alison blinked and looked towards the window. There was no glow around the edge of the curtains. It was as though there was no window, just four walls and a roof. A cubicle. A place where the air was still and soupy, where nothing moved.

She'd heard the tapping. She'd heard the sighing.

She'd closed her eyes and covered her ears with the duvet.

Now she stared at the window, hoping for some light. Just the faintest beam, that's all she wanted. A candle. Or a mobile phone lighting up for a second and then going out.

She sat up abruptly.

Nothing.

How much longer would she be haunted by this?

Later she was forcing herself to revise for her A-levels when the doorbell sounded. It was just before eight and she was sitting at her desk. Her work was piled up in front of her: her handouts, her notes, her timed essays. On the wall was a revision timetable. She was already behind. The events of the past days had eaten into her time.

She heard her mum answering the front door.

"Ali, it's for you."

She walked downstairs. Through the open door she could see Stephen Grainger. He gave an awkward smile. He was smartly dressed, in a suit. She glanced out to the street. There was an unfamiliar car parked out there, and sitting in the driver's seat was Jonesy.

"There's something you need to know."

He stepped backwards and indicated that she should follow him. She walked out along the path until they got to her gate, where Stephen stopped.

"I'm going to the police," he said. "I've talked it over with Jonesy. He's got me a solicitor and I'm going down there now."

She didn't know what to say. It was unexpected. It was a shock.

"I know we said we wouldn't ever do this, but it looks like Jackson might actually go and confess, and then it's going to be worse for me than anyone else. You know that's true. With my record and my age and the fact that I was driving."

"I know."

"So if I go and tell them what happened, it looks like I'm going of my own free will and it'll go better for me when it comes to court."

She didn't know what to say. She found herself staring at his scar, faded now, hardly noticeable, like a line drawn with a faint pencil.

"I've phoned Jackson and told him. Obviously, as soon as I start talking, the police will know who I was with. Jonesy's solicitor says that they will interview me and then let me go. They'll probably give me a date for a further interview, and it might go on like that for days or weeks until they actually charge me."

"Are you sure about this?" she said.

"Jonesy's solicitor said that it might not be looked at so seriously. A few kids involved in a row that went wrong. He thinks that you will get away with community service."

"You'll go to prison?" she said.

Stephen shook his head decisively. "No. He thinks, because I'm going along voluntarily, that I'll get a Suspended. Two years, maybe. That's why I'm going. I want to put this thing behind me. You shouldn't take too much time to make your mind."

"I've got my exams," she said, stupidly.

He shrugged. "Your choice. I'm just letting you know what I'm doing."

"Will you lose your job?" she said, almost in a whisper.

He didn't answer. He gave her a look that implied that it was a foregone conclusion. Then he went out of the gate and back to Jonesy's car.

"What did Stephen want?" her mum said, when she went into the house.

"Nothing."

"At this time of the morning?"

Alison shrugged.

"You're not getting back with him, are you?"

"It's been two years, Mum!"

In her room, she picked her mobile. She saw that she had a new message.

Stephen just rang. Come round to mine and we'll talk about it. J

She didn't really have the time to go around to Jackson's. She had revision to do. She had essays to write. She had her folders to sort out and organize. She didn't have a moment to think about anything other than her exams. She had prioritized this. This was what she had to work at. So that she could go to Downing College at Cambridge. Move away from this street, this house, this room.

She looked around; her room was now bathed in bright daylight.

She thought about the noises in the night. It gave her a rush of anguish. She looked at her books. One day they would sit on a table in a room in the halls of Downing College.

Would the noises stop then?

Or would they just go on for ever?

What if she went to the police station? What would happen then? Would she be interviewed and then given a further appointment, as if she were going to the dentist for a check-up? And what would she tell the police? Stephen said she should tell them the truth. But he meant the truth as he knew it. Not *Alison's truth*. No, neither Stephen nor Jackson knew about Alison's truth. Only she knew for sure what had happened.

And she could never tell that to the police.

Later she found herself outside Jackson's. His mother answered the door. She smiled brightly and Alison assumed from this that she had no idea that her son was about to give himself up to the police

"Hello, Alison. Ryan's upstairs," she said.

Alison went up the two flights of stairs to the loft. She knocked on the door lightly and called out to Jackson.

"Hi!" he said.

She walked straight into his room and across to the bed and sat on the edge of it. He was in his jeans but he'd not yet put a top on. His feet were bare and his hair was damp.

"I'm going to the police now," he said.

"With your mum?" she said.

He shook his head. "I'm not going to tell her until after I've been. I can't cope with the upset before I've actually spoken to the police. What about you?"

"Me?"

"Will you tell your parents?"

"I don't know. I don't know if I'm going to go. I don't have to go just because Stephen has decided. . ."

Jackson stared at her. He looked as if he was trying to work her out.

"You'll have to go to the police. Stephen will say that it was the three of us. I'll have to say that it was the three of us. . ."

"I don't know. . ."

"I need to finish in the bathroom. Then we'll talk. . ." Jackson said distractedly.

She nodded and watched as he closed the bathroom door behind him. Then she stood up and walked up and down. She looked around. She'd not been in Jackson's room for two years. It was tidier. There were fewer things. The sofa had gone. In its place was a sewing machine on a small table. A chest of drawers was beside it and, on the top, an open box filled with sewing paraphernalia, reels of cotton, scissors, remnants and patterns.

They were going to the police. Today. Now.

The rest of the room was too tidy. Jackson's shelves were neat, his books stacked evenly, his CDs and DVDs all sharp angles and level surfaces. His mum must have tidied the room while he'd been away. She'd even started to use it herself. Maybe she liked to be up there *because* it was his room.

The bed was messy. The duvet had been roughly pulled up, and on the floor beside it was a rucksack that was half open, some things pulled out of it. There were two pairs of plimsolls and socks strewn about, and an iPod and mobile and the tangled wires of rechargers. In among it all was a small notebook. It was brown leather and had a piece of elastic to hold the pages tightly. It looked battered. The corners flicked up a bit. She picked it up. Some newsprint had been folded into the pages. She opened it and took the cuttings out and unfolded the top one. It was a newspaper article that must have been written the day after Daniel's body was found. TRAGEDY AT DAGENHAM. To the side of the article was a photograph of the derelict car park. At the bottom of the article was a tiny photograph of a container. It gave her a curdling feeling to look at it. Behind it was another cutting. TEENAGE BOY ENTOMBED. It had a photograph of Harry's Diner.

The bathroom door opened and Jackson came back into the room.

"I carry those with me all the time," he said.

He sat down on the bed and pulled on some socks and trainers.

"How will you ever forget if you keep this sort of stuff?"

He pulled a T-shirt on and came across to the bedside cabinet and picked up his things: wallet, phone, coins.

"That's the point, though," he said. "I don't *want* to forget."

They got off the bus and walked towards the police station.

"Do you think they'll arrest us?" she said.

He nodded. "The least we can expect is perverting the course of justice; the most is manslaughter. I looked into it when I was in Brighton. One of the guys who lived in my brother's house was a law student. I put this hypothetical case to them."

"Manslaughter," Alison said weakly, coming to a stop on the pavement.

Slaughter. The very word was harsh. She leaned against a shop window. *Slaughter*: it suggested a violent death; much drama, much blood, the snuffing out of a boy's life. She began to shake. Her hands trembled and she clamped them to her sides.

Jackson put his arm around her and spoke quietly. "This is the beginning of the end of this whole awful thing. There's no living with this. I've tried for two years. I don't know how you've managed. You seem so closed up, so tight, so boxed off from everything. You can't mean to go on like that? We have to get this out, tell people. Then they can think the worst of us, the absolute worst of us. We can go to rock bottom."

"My parents?" she said, a swooning feeling taking over her.

"Let them know the worst. Then, only then, can we start coming back up again, getting out of this hole that we've dug for ourselves."

"I don't know. . ." she said.

"Come on," he said, pulling her arm gently.

She started to walk again.

They were going to tell the police. Jackson was going to tell them everything. Let them think the worst, he'd said, but she couldn't do that.

"Stephen's got his own solicitor. We'll have a duty solicitor."

"Will they call my mum and dad?" she said.

"Only if you want. You're over sixteen. You can be interviewed without a parent. You will have to tell them eventually."

She nodded. But not yet. It may be possible to put off telling them for a while, for weeks maybe, so that she could do her exams and get ready for Cambridge. Her exams. Would she still be able to do her exams? And go to Cambridge? They were coming up to the station and Alison felt a sense of dread, her steps becoming more hesitant. Jackson went ahead of her. He virtually ran up to the main doors and pressed the intercom button. A buzz sounded and he pushed the heavy glass door open.

She looked in at the interior of the building. The ceiling was low; it felt as though she might scrape the top of her head along it.

"It's only a few steps. Then the last couple of years will really be in the past."

She let Jackson edge her into the station, and she stood with him at the counter. One of the officers behind the glass looked up.

"We're here to talk to an officer. About something ... about a crime that was committed two years ago. About this case." He slipped the newspaper cutting on to the counter. The words stared up at them. TRAGEDY AT DAGENHAM. "We have information about it."

"Take a seat, son," the man said, looking interested. "Someone'll come and see you soon."

They sat down as the man disappeared through a door. The other officer craned his neck to look at them. Jackson was still holding the leather book in his hand. Sticking out of it was the other newspaper cutting. She reached across and took it out of the pages. TEENAGE BOY ENTOMBED. She looked at the photograph of the container. It wasn't the actual container, not *their* container. It was just an example.

She'd seen that container again.

She'd been to that very place on Thursday, 24th June, two years before. She remembered it as though it was yesterday. Five days after they left him there. The day before the leavers' assembly. The day before they found his body.

She'd been there on her own and no one had ever known about it.

Now, in the police station, she heard some noise from behind the counter and there was movement as the other policeman came back. A door opened and an older man walked out of it. He was wearing a dark suit and rimless glasses. He looked smart and in charge. Around his neck was an identity tag with his photo. It reminded Alison of Stephen's work tag and her own, in her bag at home. They were just annoying little badges that had to hang around the neck, and yet they represented normality, a job, a role, a place in the world. What place would any of them have now?

The man stared at both of them. Jackson stood up uncertainly. Alison sat where she was.

"And you are?" the man said.

"Ryan Jackson, and this is Alison Rose."

The man nodded before he'd even said the names, as though he knew, and he'd been expecting them to come. Just then the door opened again and a WPC came out. It was Emma Myers, the girl with the white hair who'd come to see her two years before. Now her hair wasn't white but brown. Neither did she look so young, so fresh-faced. She stood next to the plain-clothes policeman and didn't make eye contact with her. She gave off a coldness which suggested that she'd already heard what Stephen had to say.

"OK, we'll take you first, Mr Jackson. And meanwhile WPC Myers will find somewhere for you to sit, Miss Rose."

Jackson walked off behind the man and Alison stood up and looked sheepishly at Emma Myers. The WPC gave no sign of recognition. There was even something haughty about her, as if she was upset that she'd been lied to two years before.

"This way," she said.

Alison followed her deeper into the police station.

TWENTY-SIX

Year Eleven

It had been four whole days since they'd killed Daniel.

Sunday. Monday. Tuesday. Wednesday.

Ali walked distractedly up and down. She was out of control. The visit from the police was supposed to put an end to it, but it hadn't.

When her mum came in from work she must have heard her crying because she ran straight up the stairs to her room.

"What's happened?" her mum said, reaching out and grabbing hold of her arm.

She put her hand over her eyes. They were wet; her face was hot. Her emotions were out of control. She was trying to hold her mind together and her body was wilting and collapsing. She felt herself shaking and sobbing. How long had she been doing that? Her mum clucked and pulled at her arm and led her along the landing and into the bathroom. She could hear her mum's voice, but it was as though it was far away. She heard the tap water running and felt her mum manoeuvre her so that she was sitting on the edge of the bath. Then she felt a warm, wet flannel patting her eyes and her mum's arm around her.

"Whatever's the matter?" her mum said.

"Daniel..." she started.

"You're upset about that poor boy who's gone missing?"

Her dad had come into the bathroom by then and was looking embarrassed at the emotional scene. She went to speak but the words got lost amid snuffles. Later, she heard her mum talking to her dad in the next bedroom.

"She's still upset about that missing boy," her mum said.

"No word about him, then?" her dad said.

"I feel for his dad. Not knowing what's happened to his son. Whether he's tried to kill himself again. Poor man. What must he be going through!"

In her room she sat rigidly on her bed. Her tears had dried up. How simple she had thought it would be. To *confess*. But instead of sending a stern-looking man, a proper policeman, they'd sent her a girl, just out of college; someone not dissimilar to her. How could she tell this girl about what they'd done?

Now Daniel would stay where he was. Mr Feeny, who had thanked them in a letter, who had given the school a thousand pounds, would still not know what had happened to his son, who'd been missing for four days.

She went to bed early. She didn't get undressed; she just lay on top of the duvet. The window was open and from outside she could hear the sound of people in their back gardens talking, laughing, some distant music. Someone was having a party or a barbecue.

There were times when she almost slept, but something in her head nagged at her, kept her tossing and turning. She heard the house go quiet and the noise from the back gardens subside. She heard her mum and dad go to bed, her mum calling out, "You OK, Ali?" She listened as the house finally stilled. She dozed

190

and jerked awake again. She turned over and stared at the bedroom wall, at the flat surface, now darkly coloured. It sent her into a kind of trance and she stayed like that for a long time.

In the deep night, just after three, she noticed the first signs of light. She could make out the window ledge and the folds of the curtain. She lay and watched as the room slowly emerged from the blackness: the desk and chair, the television screen, the wardrobe. Her eyes got used to the greys and she sat up and turned on the bedside light. She picked up her mobile. She considered sending Jackson a message. *I didn't tell the police anything.* He would be relieved. She, on the other hand, would feel wretched, useless, cowardly. And Daniel was still lying in that container because of it.

After a while she sat up.

She could change that. That one thing *could* be changed.

Instead of sending Jackson a message, she could ring the police and tell them where Daniel's body was. She could make an anonymous phone call. That was all it took. She could wait until daylight and slip out and go up to the broadway and use a call box.

She could do that one thing. She could.

At just before five she got up. She crept round her room. She checked that her purse had coins in it. She pulled out a hooded sweatshirt from her drawer. Being as quiet as she could, she went down the stairs, and without making a sound, she opened the front door and went out. She carefully pulled it behind her so that it only made a click when it shut.

It was cool outside. There was no one around. She put her head down and walked along. She didn't look at Stephen's house. At times she felt like breaking into a run, but she didn't. A phone call. That was all it took. Mr Feeny had a right to know what had happened to his son.

She got to the broadway. The only movement she could see was a couple of men smoking outside the minicab office. It looked like their cars were parked alongside, waiting for early-morning fares.

She headed for the station, where she knew there were payphones. She stepped inside a booth. She got her money out. Then she stopped. What was she going to say?

There's a dead body in a container in the yard behind Harry's Diner.

There's a container in the old Ford car park in Dagenham. There's a dead body in it.

A boy's been killed. His body's in a container opposite the Ford factory.

She held the receiver and looked hopelessly around. Her eyes stopped when she saw the camera. Across the road, fixed up high on the wall of a fast-food shop, was a CCTV camera. It was pointing straight at her. She turned her back on it but then saw that opposite her, above the entrance to the station, was another. This one seemed to move, as if someone was working it. She replaced the receiver and walked away.

She went towards the minicabs. The drivers looked expectantly at her. She pulled her purse out and checked. She had a ten-pound note. It was enough.

"Opposite the Ford factory. There's a café there called Harry's Diner?"

"I know it. Not sure it'll be open yet," a driver said, frowning, dropping his dog-end on to the pavement and walking round the front of the car.

He dropped her outside.

"Are you sure you're all right?" he said.

She nodded and he gave her some change and then drove off.

The dual carriageway seemed misty. The empty road stretched away from her, out towards the Queen Elizabeth Bridge. She felt cold and put her hood up and turned to look at Harry's Diner.

The lights were off in the café. There was no one around. She skirted the building and walked into the yard behind. She steeled herself for the moment when she would glimpse the container.

It was at the other end of the lot. A brown, metal rectangle.

It sat solid and unyielding.

Inside, it held a dead boy.

Her stomach dropped. A sense of dread washed through her. It ran along her veins. Her arms and legs seemed to hum with it.

She was about to step forward when she saw, in the far corner, a man with two black dogs. One was loose, sniffing round at the ground; the other was on a lead and had a muzzle on. The man had his back to her, so she stepped behind the side of the café. Moments later she looked back out and saw that the man and his dogs were heading off, away from the car park.

There was no one else around. She walked into the car park, towards the container. It seemed a long way away. The only other times that she had been there had been in Stephen's car. Now, as she walked, she was aware of the distance. Something moved at the corner of her eye. She stopped and looked round. A rat disappeared between the plastic bags of rubbish that had been left there.

She looked anxiously around at the other stuff: the van, the crates, the banks of weeds that had shot up through the broken tarmac and concrete. What other things were hidden there?

There was some wire fencing around the petrol pumps that she hadn't noticed before. On it was a sign that said *Trespassers Will Be Prosecuted*. She passed it and walked another ten or twelve steps and stopped. The container was ten metres or so away. She could see the side of it where the door had been hanging open. She could see behind it, where the wire fencing had held up. Beyond it was open land, a scrubby, grassy area that filled the gap between a housing estate and the old car park. The nearest building was a pub about a hundred metres away. She'd seen none of this on the nights that Stephen had driven her there. In her mind, this place had just been the back lot of a café they sometimes used. She had had no notion of it being a smaller bit of a bigger landscape.

She resumed her steps. She kept looking round to see if anyone was about. It was just after five. She pulled the strings of her hood, tightening it round her neck. Another few metres and she found herself within a hand's reach of the rusted metal walls.

How could Daniel's life have ended here?

Her mouth filled up and she swallowed back. Weeks ago she had helped *save* his life. How could it be that for four and a half days his body had been in this oversized coffin?

She put her hand out to touch the metal.

Sorry, she wanted to say. *Sorry, sorry*. She let her face fall forward so that she was flat against the side. She felt the gritty surface scraping her skin. *I'm so, so sorry*.

Then she heard a knock.

She opened her eyes. There it was. A faint knock.

She stepped back. She looked around. She listened for the sound of a car coming along into the yard, but there was nothing.

She heard it again. A knocking sound. No, a tapping sound.

She stood completely still and stared at the rusted wall of the container.

Tap.

She put her arm out and stiffened her fingers so that they touched the flaky metal.

Tap.

It was inside. The sound was coming from *inside* the container.

"What?" she croaked.

Tap.

She stepped back. She was mistaken. It was coming from somewhere else. Someone in a garden somewhere was working on something metal. They were tapping; metal on metal. The sound was carrying across the empty ground. It seemed close but it was coming from far away.

Then she heard the moan.

Pitiful like a dog.

Her heart seemed to pause. Her body was rigid. She looked in horror at the metal wall, at the ridges, at the brown colour broken up with bubbles of paint, and then when the sound came again it cut through her like a thin pointed knife.

A cry.

She stepped sideways. She looked frantically around. Not a soul. Not a soul. She tried to move quickly but her legs were weak, her shoes heavy. She seemed to be stumbling like a drunk. She made herself stand completely still and took a great breath, as though she'd been underwater.

Then she walked across to the place where the black dogs had been earlier and stepped on to the open ground. In moments she was running. She didn't stop. She ran and ran and ran.

TWENTY-SEVEN

That day she was dazed.

She went home and closed her bedroom door and lay staring at the ceiling. Her mum came in and went out. She didn't feel well, she said. Her dad put his head round the door. She was ill. There was whispering in the hallway, but they left her alone. Both of them went to work. She lay in bed all morning, but there was no sleep.

She left a note for her mum and dad and went to her gran's.

Her gran's carer was there when she arrived, hanging up some washing on the line. While her gran was drinking tea, she went into the garden and got out the lawnmower. Mowing took her almost two hours. Up and down the grass, making sure that the edge of the mower lined up with the previously mowed track. Up and down, she kept her arms stretched out fully, all her strength pushing into the mower to move it up to the end of the garden so that she could turn round and mow back towards the house.

Eventually it was finished.

The muscles in her arms felt stiff, but she didn't care.

Her gran was watching a quiz show.

"Hello, Alison," the old lady said, as if she'd just arrived.

She sat down. It was almost five. Just over an hour until she'd asked her dad to come for her. The quizmaster was getting ready to ask his next question. Her gran was staring at the screen. Ali wondered what she was seeing, what she was understanding. The contestant was looking puzzled, tapping his fingers on the side of his forehead as if that might dislodge the answer. "I know it," he said, "I just can't think." And then, as if the answer had popped up in his head, he said, "1968!" There was applause and the man looked pleased with himself. Her gran looked at her and smiled. Maybe she understood some of it.

"You know what, Gran? Something horrible happened last Saturday night."

Her gran was staring at the television screen.

"This boy got killed."

The quizmaster was asking a new question.

"At least I thought he'd got killed. There was this argument. Over a girl? And this boy hit his head when he fell. Then we all got in a panic and we left him inside this metal container."

Her gran turned away from the television screen and looked at her. Her gran's eyes were green but they looked filmy, opaque, as if she were looking at her through frosted glass.

"And this is the worst bit. *He wasn't dead*."

Her gran seemed puzzled. Behind her, on the television screen, the contestant had got out of his chair and was dancing around.

"We didn't know it," she whispered, "but he was *still alive*."

Her gran was staring at her. Her eyebrows creased. Was she understanding?

"Don't cry, Alison," she said, patting her arm.

But Ali did cry. She pulled out a tissue and blew her nose and cried softly for as long as the programme was on. Her gran fussed over Rex and a different programme came on and Ali went upstairs to the bathroom to wash her face.

When her dad arrived, Rex jumped up and down.

"All right, Mum? Feeling better, Ali?"

Ali gave a stiff nod. Her dad leaned down and gave her gran a kiss on the cheek. Then he went straight to the table and picked up Gran's letters and began to roughly tear them open and sort through them. Later, when he'd checked around the house to make sure everything was OK, they got ready to leave.

"We'll see you, Sunday, Mum," her dad said.

Her gran nodded, her eyes drawn back to the television screen.

Ali bent over to give her a kiss on the cheek.

"Don't cry any more, Alison," her gran said, her fingers clasping Ali's wrist tightly.

"OK, Gran," she said, rubbing the old lady's arm, feeling her papery skin and the bones in her knuckles.

Jackson was at her house when she got back. He was in the living room.

"Hi," he said guardedly, standing up as she came in.

"What's up?" she said, closing the door so that her mum or dad couldn't hear what was being said.

"Have you seen the police?" he said.

She nodded.

"Did you tell them?"

She was confused. Tell them? Then she remembered. He meant the interview with the WPC. He was still thinking about her confessing to the police about last Saturday night. *Almost five days before.* He had no idea that she had moved on from that.

She shook her head.

He sat down on her sofa and put his head in his hands.

She watched with dismay. Was he crying? He wiped his eyes with the back of his hand and she saw that the leather band was still there, laced on to his arm. Her band was upstairs. She'd not worn it since before the weekend.

She stepped across and sat down beside him.

"I thought we'd be arrested," he said.

He was like a child that had to be comforted. She put her arm around his shoulders. He was hot, feverish almost. She pulled him into her chest and after a moment or two he put his arms around her. They sat slumped against the end of the sofa for what seemed like a long time. She let her mind go blank. For the first time that day she felt calm. There, amid the scatter cushions, she felt a lightness come over her. She sensed her mum and dad were next door, in the kitchen. The radio was on and she could feel their movements through the floorboards.

She was still. She could feel her heart beating softly, unhurried.

If only they could stay together like this.

But Jackson gave a shudder. She stroked his back. After a few moments she found herself saying things she should have said days ago.

"I thought you liked me," she said, her voice hardly louder than a whisper.

She felt him turn slightly.

"I do like you," he said, his breath hot on her chest.

"No, I mean, I thought you really liked me. That you *wanted* me."

He sat up. He looked puzzled.

"When you were with Hannah and then you broke up. I thought that you would come to me."

"I did like you. I *do* like you."

"So why didn't you come to me? When Hannah broke up with you?"

"You were with Stephen."

She shook her head. "I'd finished with Stephen. I told you that."

"But it was only days before," he said. "I didn't want it to look as though I was jumping in. I didn't want it to seem like *that* to Stephen. I respect Stephen. He's a good bloke."

Respect. It was such an important word for Jackson.

"You could have told me. I came to see you. I sent you a text. Why didn't you tell me what you felt?"

He sat up and moved back from her. "That would have been just as bad. To tell you. Like you and me had a secret against Stephen. I just thought it was better to let a couple of weeks go by."

"I thought that you didn't care. . ."

"I was going to wait. I didn't know about Hannah at the time, but even then I wouldn't have done anything."

He meant he didn't know about Hannah and Daniel.

"There's no way I could have done that to Stephen."

If she'd just waited. For a week or two. Just been patient.

"I do like you. I've always liked you," he said.

He kissed her. At first it was slow and awkward. When he

201

pulled her close, she was unsure. She tried to move away.

How could she kiss him now after what they had done?

He kept going, though, and she found herself sinking into the kiss, moving her head one way and then another. She put her arms around him and felt him clutching at her, pulling her close so that she could hardly move. In the back of her head she could hear her mum and dad in the kitchen, the radio tuned to a music station that was playing old-fashioned songs.

She felt herself easing backwards so that he seemed to be pinning her down. She edged her legs up on to the sofa and he moved with her.

Hadn't she wanted this?

Wasn't this what it had all been about? Having Jackson for herself.

She was moaning, making low sounds. Pleasure was tingling through her and it didn't matter that they were bruised – damaged, even – by what had happened. Because, in the end, that's what it had all been about. Loving Jackson.

He stopped suddenly. She felt the kiss taken from her mouth. He looked at her strangely and pulled himself away. He sat back along the sofa, looking concerned. She felt the chill of him moving away.

Then she realized she was crying.

"I'm sorry, I'm sorry. I thought you wanted this," he said.

"I do," she said, "I do want it."

"Everything's messed up. You and me, it's all messed up."

He stood up.

"Wait," she said, wanting to open up to him. "This morning I went back. . ."

"No, I get it. Everything's different. You, me, Stephen. Nothing will ever be the same for us."

"No, listen, I went down to the place, the car park. I went there, this morning. . ."

But he wasn't listening. He'd walked out of the room. She was still sitting on the sofa as the front door closed behind him. The sound of music came from the kitchen and she heard her mum's voice above a quiet bit of the song.

She lay back on the sofa, weak and nauseated. She pushed her face into the cushion. In the dark she saw a boy lying inside a metal box, tapping on the side in the hope that someone would hear him; that someone would get him out.

TWENTY-EIGHT

Ali turned up early for the leavers' assembly.

She'd been first that morning at the charity shop. She'd got there fifteen minutes before opening time and had to stand at the locked door and wait for Mrs Lumsden to get there. It wasn't that she'd miscalculated the time it would take. It was that she'd got up early, got dressed and had breakfast quickly. What was the point of hanging round the house? *Hanging round* gave her time to think, and she didn't want that, so she set off as soon as she could. Mrs Lumsden was delighted to see her and offered her a cup of coffee before they started work, but Ali wanted to get going and start sorting things out immediately.

The leavers' assembly started at two. She arrived half an hour before. She went to the garden area and sat on one of the benches. She was the first year eleven student to get there. She was wearing jeans and a top, nothing special. She knew that the other kids would be dressed in their best. Any chance to show off before leaving. There would be lashings of make-up, more than normal to aggravate the teachers. The skirts would be short and the jeans tight. There would be midriffs showing, low necklines. There would be nose studs and masses of jewellery. The boys would be aloof and shiny-looking. They might wear box-fresh trainers and just-washed jeans. There were always exceptions.

The hippy types would roll in wearing floating skirts and flat sandals, and the funereal ones, all in black, would stand in small groups like crows gathering on a summer's day.

Ali had seen it all last year when she'd been helping set up the assembly. She'd sat back and smiled at the way the year eleven girls came in all self-conscious, brushing down their clothes, looking at their nails, stealing glances at each other, checking out what everyone else was wearing. The boys had strutted in looking like frisky dogs. They stood in small groups, crying out in delight when someone new arrived, as if they hadn't seen them for months.

That lunch time Ali had picked up the first thing that came to hand. Her mum had looked oddly at her. "Are you wearing those old clothes?" she'd said. Ali nodded tersely. She wasn't making a statement. She was just getting by. Doing the things she had to do. Going into school, seeing Gran, doing housework, going to the charity shop. All of these things helped to pass the time. Like eating meals, one mouthful after another. None of it tasted of anything.

After Jackson had left, she'd had all evening to make a phone call to the police. She'd already wasted a day, but she could still have done it. *Make the phone call. End it all.* But she hadn't done it.

Why not?

Because she was *fearful* of what they would find.

A boy who had lain there for five days. A boy who hadn't eaten or drunk or maybe even moved. A boy who'd tapped a message of despair on to a metal wall.

Why hadn't she told anyone?

She'd been afraid.

Behind the door of the container was some terrible half-dead lad who would stare at them through dehydrated eyes. She and

Stephen and Jackson would have to look at his dry skin and his blinking eyes as he pointed his filthy finger at them. Then the world would know what they had done, how they had left him to die. They hadn't meant it to happen. They'd thought he was already dead, but no one would believe them.

Now she was sitting waiting for the leavers' assembly.

She was calm.

More kids joined her in the school garden. Some were from her class and they came over and stood around her. "Hi, Ali," they said and began talking amongst themselves. She looked round for Hannah but couldn't see her. Would Jackson come?

"Hi, Ali," one of the lads said, sidestepping her and walking across to some other kids.

All of a sudden the garden seemed to be swamped with year elevens. The smell of perfume and aftershave was strong. The voices were many, the girls' fluttering above and the boys' growling below. There were so many kids that she couldn't see through them and could no longer tell whether Jackson was there or not. A few moments later she could hear the hand-rung bell and she looked to see one of the teachers holding it awkwardly by the entrance to the hall.

They filed in. She waited till the very end. Jackson definitely wasn't there. She followed and sat herself in the back row at the end so that she could get away when it was all over.

Get away to what? She had nowhere to go and no one to see.

Everyone was talking lowly. At the front of the hall was a long wooden table with a bowl of flowers on each end. It looked like an altar, but instead of a cross, it had a CD player in the middle playing light orchestral music. This would go on for a while, and then Mrs Caine and the deputy head of year would come in and start the final assembly. They would all be asked to shake hands with the person next to them and wish them well. Ali looked to her side and saw a girl from another class who she'd never spoken to. What did it matter who she shook hands with?

The swinging doors opened and Mrs Caine walked in. Close behind her was the deputy head of year, and following on were two more senior teachers. Ali frowned. The doors swung back and forth for a few moments and looked as though they might settle when one of them opened gingerly and a WPC came in. She had taken her hat off and was looking grave.

It was Emma Myers, the policewoman who had visited her at her house.

Ali felt herself sinking into her seat. With her hands she held the tops of the legs of the chair. The rest of the kids were going quiet, and there was just the odd mumble and beep of a mobile phone. Mrs Caine made a sweeping gesture with her hand so that one of the teachers turned off the CD player and the hall was instantly quiet. The silence was stark. Ali was staring at the scene, her throat clenched.

Mrs Caine coughed. Emma Myers stood to the side and was looking down at a pad that was in her hands.

"Good afternoon, year eleven. I'm going to come straight to the point and tell you that your leaving assembly has been cancelled."

There was a moan.

"I have some very bad news for you. Some very sad news."

There was an expectant air of quiet.

"All of you will remember Daniel Feeny..."

Another moan filtered around the room. A number of shushes

sounded, and Mrs Caine looked ferociously around the entire seated area. People shuffled in their seats and there were a few grumpy looks, but no one made a sound.

"I had some very bad news today. You will remember that Daniel went missing almost a week ago and we were very concerned about him. It seems . . . it appears . . . that there has been a terrible accident. . ."

Mrs Caine coughed again and her eye caught the policewoman's. Ali watched as some kind of telepathic message passed between the pale young woman and the shocked teacher.

"Daniel's body was found today down by the Ford factory in Dagenham. It looks as though he was injured and became trapped and it appears, although no one is completely sure yet, that he has been in this place for some time."

No one spoke.

"Daniel's family are naturally very shocked about this, and although we are not a church school, I would ask you all to give a minute's silence, during which time you may think about Daniel or pray for him, whatever gives you most comfort."

Mrs Caine stopped speaking and looked down at the ground. The deputy head of year clasped his hands together and closed his eyes and his lip began to move. Emma Myers stared straight ahead. The students sat stiffly. Ali didn't know if they were taking it seriously, but no one broke the silence. She closed her eyes but made her mind go blank. When she opened them again, she was unsettled to see Emma Myers staring straight at her.

She felt heavy with guilt. Yesterday he had still been alive.

Now Daniel was dead and his suffering was over.

She knew, though, that hers had only just begun.

TWENTY-NINE

Year Thirteen

The police station was a big building. The room Alison was sitting in was on the second floor. It didn't look like an interview room. She'd seen them on police dramas on television. They were small and square and had two-way mirrors where other officers sat and watched the interview. There was usually a table with chairs on either side, and on the table, a tape recorder.

This room looked like a meeting room of some sort. There was carpet and big windows and a circular table that had six chairs around it. On one of the walls was an interactive whiteboard.

The WPC had left her on her own for a few moments. She would be back soon, she said.

She wondered where the others were.

Stephen would be in an interview room. Maybe his solicitor was sitting beside him and Jonesy was waiting outside. Jackson would be with the man with the rimless glasses. He would be keen to talk it all out, to get it off his chest, and the detective would sit passively and listen without expression, his eyes cold behind his invisible lenses.

Soon someone would come and talk to Alison.

In her hands she saw that she still had Jackson's cutting. TEENAGE BOY ENTOMBED. She flattened it out on the table. She remembered reading it in the days after Daniel's body had been found, when the police were asking questions of everyone who knew him. She'd read all the reports, everything she could lay her hands on. Day after day, for weeks.

There'd been no flowers, she remembered.

In other cases of public death, there were usually flowers pinned to a fence or bunches leaned against a garden wall; sometimes they were tied to a tree at the side of the road, or plants in flowerpots were placed next to tea-light candles, cards and notes in plastic covers to stop them being soaked by the rain.

But there'd been no flowers for Daniel. The place, the derelict car park, had been too out of the way. Hardly anyone walked past it to get anywhere. The café in front of it was only used by drivers and passing trade. She'd seen one person near it, a dog-walker. Stephen had said he'd seen some homeless types using the container during the winter. But no one walked across the pitted tarmac and placed a bouquet of lilies for Daniel Feeny.

The door opened and a woman walked in with WPC Emma Myers. The woman was older, quite stout, with grey hair at the front and glasses on a chain resting on her chest. A man followed her. He was wearing a checked jacket and dark trousers. There were a number of pens in his top pocket and he was carrying a briefcase that looked too heavy. He seemed to slope to one side.

"We're ready for you now, Miss Rose. This is Mr Briggs, the duty solicitor. If you'll just follow me."

Alison stood up wearily.

The first part of the interview stopped after an hour. WPC Emma Myers and the older woman, Detective Crabtree, went out. Moments later a male officer brought in two cups of coffee on a tray with twists of sugar and plastic thimbles of milk. Alison drank hers down in moments, feeling the hot liquid scalding her throat. Mr Briggs, the solicitor, talked quietly to her, outlining the scheme of what would happen. He repeated the things that Stephen had said to her earlier that day. There would be more interviews, and eventually the police and the Crown Prosecution Service would decide which charges to bring.

Would she go to prison?

Mr Briggs thought that she wouldn't, but he didn't want to commit himself. Mr Briggs thought she should tell her parents as soon as possible.

The two police officers came back into the room. Emma Myers was holding a pad. Detective Crabtree had an envelope file. It was grey and had no labels on it. It looked brand spanking new and was thin, as though it contained nothing at all.

She turned the recorder on.

Then they started again, going over the story, repeating

times and places and who said what. Alison was tired. She answered everything from memory. She didn't have to take a moment to think about it. She didn't leave anything out. She hadn't forgotten a single word that was said that night.

Eventually the questions became softer and more general. What was the weather like? What was the traffic like? What were you wearing?

They were winding down the interview. Detective Crabtree was glancing at her watch. Emma Myers was quiet. She hadn't said much. Alison thought that she'd been making some notes, but when she placed her pad face up, Alison saw that it was covered in doodles.

"We'll see Miss Rose again tomorrow morning," Detective Crabtree said.

The solicitor was putting the tops back on two of his pens and sliding them into his top pocket. The interview felt like it was over, but when Alison looked at the recording machine, it still showed a red light.

WPC Emma Myers leaned forward and spoke.

"Just before you go, there's something else we wanted to raise with you."

Mr Briggs stopped packing his stuff up. Alison frowned.

"An odd thing happened in the old car park on the day before Daniel's body was discovered."

"You may or may not be aware," Detective Crabtree said, "that after a year, we reviewed the case again. We were lucky enough to get a spot on a television programme and we appealed for sightings of anything unusual down by the Ford factory in those days after June 19th."

Alison sat very still.

"It's an out-of-the-way place, so we didn't get much of a response. We only had a couple of significant phone calls from members of the public. One was from a man walking his dogs on the morning of Thursday, 24th June. Another was from a cab driver, and that was also about the morning of Thursday, 24th June."

Alison looked at Emma Myers. She noticed how her lips looked thin and there were blemishes on her cheeks: raised veins, maybe brought out by the extreme cold or hot weather. When she first met Emma, she'd thought that there wasn't much difference in their ages, but now she definitely looked older, worn down.

Detective Crabtree had put her glasses on and was tracing a line along the flap of the new grey folder with her finger. Emma Myers carried on talking.

"The cab driver said he drove a young girl down to the docks that morning. A girl of about sixteen, he thought, with brown hair. She'd been wandering about the broadway early in the morning. He dropped her off about five-thirty, he thought. Now here's where it gets odd. A man walking his dogs on the car park said he thought he saw a young man wearing a hoodie standing by the café at about five o'clock. He said he thought it was someone relieving himself. He only mentioned it, he said, because some moments later the young man in the hoodie was standing in front of the container where the boy's body was found a day later."

Alison looked from one to the other. She turned to her solicitor.

"I'm tired," she said.

"There was no CCTV footage on the site, so it wasn't possible to pick up any images. However, we did look at some cameras on the broadway round about five-fifteen, and we picked up this image."

Detective Crabtree pushed the grey folder to the WPC and she opened it and pulled out an A4 photograph. She laid it flat on the table and pushed it towards Alison.

The image was grainy. It was taken from a camera that was high up and at an angle. It showed a blurry profile of Alison. Her hair was flat on her head and her face was a distance away but it was her. Not that anyone else would have been able to identify it.

"You may notice that the person in this photograph is wearing a black hoodie, although the hood is down. The question is, why should this person have gone to the car park and stood by the container that Daniel was eventually found in?"

Detective Crabtree turned off the recording machine. The clicking sound broke Alison's reverie and she looked up, blinking, as if she'd been in the dark and someone had just turned the light on. WPC Myers plucked the photo from her hand and fed it back into the folder.

"That's all for today, Mr Briggs. We'll see your client at ten tomorrow morning. Unless, of course, there's anything she wants to talk about before then. Here's my card with my mobile number."

She threw a card on the table. It was blue with black print on it. Then she stood up. Emma Myers stood up. Mr Briggs stood up, pulling his weighty briefcase off the floor.

Only Alison stayed sitting down.

As she was leaving the police station, she heard a beep on her mobile. She had a message. She stood still while she read it. It was from Jackson.

My first interview is over. I don't have to go back until next week. Let me know how yours went.

She felt tears on her face. She wiped her cheeks with her sleeve. How weak and useless crying was. It achieved nothing and changed nothing. Her skin was raw with the constant wetting and wiping. She looked up as she was rubbing her eyes. At a second-floor window of the police station, she saw the face of Emma Myers. It gave her a start.

She walked off.

THIRTY

Alison walked through the shopping area. She had plans. She knew exactly what she was going to do. She went to the bus stop and waited. The electronic screen said it was six minutes until her bus. She'd have to get off a stop early in order to get what she wanted. The street was busy with people hurrying here and there. The traffic was in a line inching forward, past the station.

It was the same bus stop where she'd first seen Hannah and Daniel together that day, two years before. She'd been working in the charity shop and looked out of the window and saw them sitting on the funny half seats of the shelter. Daniel had kissed Hannah and that's when she'd known for sure that they were together.

Hannah had told her, *I never really knew him before. I like him.* Hannah hadn't had long with Daniel – a week? Ten days? Had she really got to know him? Was it possible that she could have had an effect on the odd boy who had hung around the corners of their classroom for years? Might she have relaxed him, made him less sharp and vulnerable? Might he have joined the crowd up at Blackwood, swigging back a can of lager, laughing at a joke someone had made?

No one would ever know.

What would Hannah think when she knew the whole story? *You might be going to Cambridge University and I might be working in a hairdresser's, but I'm not stupid.* No, Hannah with her big bag and her hair tongs wasn't stupid.

They hadn't been friends, not really, but along with the disgust and horror, Hannah would also feel a sort of *betrayal.*

She looked across the road at the charity shop. She could see Mrs Lumsden fussing about near the window display. The front of the shop had been painted recently and the sign had new lettering: *St Mark's Hospice.* When she'd started working there, for weeks or months maybe, she had had no idea what hospice meant. It had sounded like *hospital* to her; a place of healing. The word was soft and whispery. It made her think of people recovering from operations, and whenever she received mail or saw the words printed out, it gave her a good feeling. When she'd realized that a *hospice* was actually a place people went to in order to die, she'd been shaken.

The bus came round the corner suddenly and sped up to the stop. She waited her turn and then got on it and saw that it was almost full. She stood by a window and looked out as it rushed down the bus lane, past the standing traffic. Beside her was a woman with a baby. The baby looked dopey, its eyelids heavy, as if it was just about to drop off to sleep. The woman looked contented. She pulled a paper bag out of the pouch on the pushchair. She put her fingers in and took out a pair of earrings that were still attached to a square of card. A big ruby-coloured stone sat at the centre of each and was fringed with purple and pink beads. They glittered as the light splashed off them, and the woman smiled to herself. Alison caught her eye as she looked up.

"Just bought them," the woman said. "A bit over the top, but still. . ."

Alison nodded genially, but inside she was washed through with sadness. The earrings would hang elegantly and would look good with casual or smart clothes. The woman's baby would make a grab for them and the woman would shake her head and laugh and pull back. They were only a pair of cheap earrings, but the sight of them filled Alison with grief for something that was lost.

She got off the bus. The garage she wanted was across the road. She walked over and pulled her purse out of her bag. She had enough money. There were two buckets that held the flowers. There were six bunches left. She picked them all up and went inside to pay. The man behind the counter looked at her strangely.

"What?" he said. "You going to a funeral?"

She walked the rest of the way to the A13 and the Ford factory. It took fifteen minutes or so. The flowers weren't heavy, but they were awkward. The base of each bunch was wet from where they'd been in the bucket, and she felt the dampness on her T-shirt. She cradled three bunches in one arm and three in the other. She caught their scent as it rose up, sweet and pungent amid the petrol fumes and the fast food places that she passed. Some people looked at her oddly, but then they just went on with their business.

She left the shopping area and walked through an estate

of houses. She was tiring, but she kept going. Up ahead was the A13. She could see the traffic queuing on the far side, the road that led into London. The sky was bright, but there were clouds gathering in the distance. She turned the corner and walked along a footpath that led to the car park and Harry's Diner. She was surprised to hear machinery and building work going on. When she came out of the footpath, she saw that a high wire fence had been erected around the old car park. There were diggers there, men in orange hats and piles of building materials round the edge.

Ali looked through the fence to the place where the container had sat. There was nothing there. The ground had been squared off and looked as though it was being prepared for foundations. A gigantic cement mixer was turning slowly, squeaking on each rotation.

Further on was a sign on the fence.

Affordable Housing for Local People.

She stopped for a moment to rest. She was perspiring and she hoped that the flowers would stay fresh. Up ahead was Harry's Diner. Still doing business even though there was building work going on.

She walked round the fence until she got to a spot that was directly in front of where the old container had been. It was the best place, she thought, clutching the flowers close to her chest.

She lowered herself to her knees. She let the flowers drop gently out of her hands. She spent a few minutes taking the cellophane and the white tissue paper from them, struggling with the elastic bands, pulling away the Sellotaped sachets of flower food. She drew it all together and scrunched it up and pushed it to the side.

Some of the men on the building stood still and watched what she was doing.

She started to arrange the flowers. They were mostly carnations and roses. Petrol station blooms. She would have liked lilies and tulips, freesias and daffodils. She would have liked pot plants and teddy bears and tea-cup candles in glass dishes. She would have liked ribbons to tie on the wire fence and cards and messages in plastic folders.

But all she had were carnations and roses, and she spent her time arranging them so that they made a show, so that from a distance someone, anyone could see that something important had happened there, down by the A13, at the back of Harry's Diner.

Then she sat down on the ground with her legs crossed and stayed like that for a long time. She put her hand in her pocket to get her mobile and found something else there. She pulled out the leather band that Jackson had given her two years before. She rubbed it between her fingers; then she put it on, taking a minute to do up the button.

She took out her mobile and composed a text to Jackson.

Please don't hate me. Maybe one day when this is all over I'll come and see you in Brighton.

Ali xx

She leaned back against the wire fence and felt some of the flowers on her neck. She breathed in their scent.

Then she pressed the *send* button.